Blown Away
Under the
Big Sky

Blown Away Under the Big Sky

John Holt

NEW PULP PRESS

Published by New Pulp Press, LLC, 926 Truman Avenue, Key West, Florida 33040, USA.

For information contact:
Publisher@NewPulpPress.com

Printed in the United States of America
Visit us on the web at www.newpulppress.com

ISBN-13: 978-1945734083 (New Pulp Press)
ISBN-10: 1945734086

For Mom and Harvey...

Blown Away
Under the
Big Sky

There was, of course, no bottom to the abyss, once she had been drawn into it. It was merely a further stage of decomposition, the inability to respond to the law of gravity. The fall was slow, almost luxurious.

From *Up Above The World* by Paul Bowles

-One-

THREE MEN IN A BOAT with plenty to drink or in this case three clowns in a 16-foot Avon raft, floating down the river on a stone-cold pretty July day is nothing special out here in south central Montana. Tens of thousands of people do it every year as they cast with wildly varying degrees of skill countless different fly patterns to the river's trout – Yellowstone cutthroat, rainbows and browns. The river is world famous and many individuals both in state and out make a very good living guiding the properly attired sports downriver – hundreds of dollars a day plus money spent on flies, lines, wildly over-priced fly rods, waders, tips, lodging, meals, drinks and so on. The once eccentric, esoteric pursuit had grown into a sometimes obnoxious child that generates big bucks in Montana.

These three were a bit different, though there were others like them roaming the state looking for a quick dollar. They were land investors, developers, and perhaps most sadly fly fishing grifters intent on closing off as much prime country and trout water from the non-wealthy as possible. They'd spun off ranches on the Boulder River to hack actors, retired TV news readers and West Coast dotcom billionaires. The three clowns in the raft made millions from this. Right now they were casting grasshopper imitations along the grassy banks in the afternoon breeze along a stretch of river east of Stillwater where the river moved away from its mountainous beginnings and out onto the northern high plains. The trio hadn't experienced much success. They weren't very good at fly fishing. The action is often desultory at best during the heat of mid-day under a cloudless sky. The sun was unrelenting. Cold beers helped some but not all that much.

"We sold 12 thousand dozen flies last year through our outlets," a fat man in his fifties and sitting in the front of the raft said. "We have the kiddie trash in Haiti tie them for pennies apiece. Material is next to nothing. Customs is no problem. We clear $15 bucks on the dozen. I'll take 180K the easy way all day long."

"It all adds up. Works for me," said the one manning the oars – fortyish, trimmed beard, khaki shorts and shirt, leather necklace holding various implements of his trade, wading sandals, fly rod company logo ball cap, silk scarf, wrap around shades and the piece de resistance, a lycra pair of leggings patterned to resembled a brook trout's color patterns. He had the yuppie fly fisher oh so hip uniform down cold. An idiot on parade. "How's the deal on Cottonwood Creek going? That's some sweet water."

The guy in back, a clone of the oarsman said "We've secured access rights from the highway stream crossing west of Yorkedale for 11 miles up the lake road from the Erick's Ranch. We're working on another eight miles on the eastern edge of our lodge property near and along Cottonwood Lake. Our outfitters and guides have been told to push this water and the stuff along Sixteen Mile Creek. Brokaw and Keaton have said that they were interested in this property, too. That's why I've been pushing so hard to upgrade and update the lodge and out buildings. The so-called moneyed elite like their premium granite kitchen counters and electronic blinds. Big time Montana ranchers. More like big time mooches. Eight million. With our eight percent that's $640,000."

The three drank more beer, expensive stuff with cutesy names and labels that ran ads on TV showing inbred subnormals drinking the stuff with a slice of orange or lime or lemon, elevator music trying to be real droning in the background. The men nattered on about money and who had the priciest car while catching more of nothing as they glided down the river until one of them hooked a large Mountain whitefish, a species native to these waters, but not the sought after trout. After a spirited fight the fish came to net. The guy rowing grabbed the fish and whacked its head on the rowing frame spraying blood on himself and the guy in front, then tossed the creature on the gravel 20 feet away. They all laughed as the whitefish writhed and flopped on the hot rocks.

"Fucking whitefish. They ought to poison them out of here" the one in front offered without considering the fact that poisoning the whitefish would do a deadly number on the trout, too..

"Agreed and let's shit can the state's stream access law while we're at it. The low lifes can fish on national forest not on prime stretches flowing through our land. BS law all the way."

A phone rang. The guy in front answered.

"We put in at Sheep Mountain and are about two-thirds of the way to the Springdale take out," he said and then listened. "Fishing's real slow. Nothing on top" and he listened some more. "That's cool. We'll meet you at the Nighthawk around eight for drinks."

He ended the connection.

"That was Ross. He's got the papers for the Sixteen mile easement."

"Things are moving right along," said the guy rowing. "I like this easy money."

"Who the hell doesn't?" said the one in the back as he lit a cigar, sucking on it like his place of business was a bus station men's room.

The three finished their beers and pitched the bottles in the river behind them, before opening more. Leinenkugel at seven bucks a six. Back in the day in Wisconsin the beer went for $.59 for a six pack. You had to be near broke and terminally hungover to buy the stuff. Now through aggressive TV marketing and cute labels yuppies pay through the nose and like it. Can't blame Leinenkugel for making a serious profit on their swill.

Out of nowhere a large bald eagle swooped down and snared the dying whitefish in its talons before screaming skyward and south towards the Beartooth Mountains hanging hazy purple and white in the distance. The three took in the acrobatics of the bird as they resumed moving downstream.

A loud buzzing rode the wind coming at them from around a bend a mile below the raft, growing steadily in intensity.

"What the hell is that?"

"Probably a Beechcraft showing some swells the river before heading to Biederbeck. More tourist fishermen. More money."

The plane rounded the bend and headed straight for them, 500 feet above the water. The craft was a vintage biplane (actually a Fokker DVII, a German fighter from WWI, but these guys didn't know that). The cowl back to the cockpit was painted maize and the fuselage was a deep blue. As the plane roared down on them it banked sharply right then back on line towards the raft. The men could see a white dragon emblazoned along the plane's side behind the pilot who was wearing a leather helmet and goggles. The three stared in amazement and a vague sense of fear as the plane nosed slightly downward and increase its speed the engines roar increasing in volume and pitch. The menacing noise echoed off the buff- and salmon-colored rock cliffs guarding the river. The biplane soared over a large, grey gravel bar growing in size daily as summer's heat and drought took its toll on the river's flow. A group of antelope fled the scene bounding over a distant sage-covered bluff. A very large trout cleared the water just in front of the raft arcing in a spray of silver before crashing back through the surface,

"What the ..."the guy in back said, but his sentence went unfinished. From less than 400 yards the flickering of twin guns mounted on top and in front of the pilot indicated the unleashing of a stream of machine gun fire that ripped up the river and tore through the raft shredding fabric and human flesh. The pilot continued firing, perhaps a 1000 rounds, soared overhead and climbed almost vertically far above the river that was now carrying three dead men - a bloody mélange of flesh, bone, hair, raft material and blasted oars. The biplane leveled out at 5,000 feet. The pilot flipped off the raft and its dead with a gloved finger, then swung the fighter's nose northeast towards the enormous emptiness of central Montana. The sound of the plane's BMW engine faded and eventually the Fokker was nothing more than a speck on the horizon, just like the eagle pulling away in the opposite direction with its fish.

On the water the strong, and blood tinted, current near the bank swept the mostly-submerged raft and the dead men into a logjam. The natural construction is a tangled prison of cottonwood and pine trees torn from the river's banks, roots and all, during the raging floods common to spring runoff when countless billions of tons of snow and ice are converted by the sun's intensity or warm spring rains into often devastating floods that last for weeks. What was left of the Avon raft and the fly fishers wedged into the wood tangle, much of the debris under the surface of the aquamarine water that pulsed and burbled as it poured its way down to join the Missouri at Fort Buford. The weathered, sun-bleached trunks and limbs looked like a mass of skeletons writhing in perpetual agony.

The sun blazed white hot in the empty sky as the summer wind pushed up the river.

***

Cocktail hour at Ray's Bleachers, a place of shelter and

companionship was owned by an eccentric and generous man named Dirt Tidrow. This was an evening event of huge social importance in Biederbeck where really "huge" things rarely happened. Derelict writers, anglers, wannabe artists and others of local insignificance gathered at the ancient mahogany bar for half-price drinks, good cigars and passable conversation. Dining was available in a subdued, sparsely appointed room some feet away. The chef had a Michelin star and was a professed drunk but the food was excellent by any standards and the prices were exceptionally reasonable. Dirt's ethereal landscape paintings hung on the walls. Moody, subtle renderings of the land here and in southern Alberta had earned him a world-wide following and lots of money, though he'd still managed to put himself in a position of filing for bankruptcy twice, the last time almost a quarter-century ago when he had to sell his house, vintage cars and cash in his investments. He claimed he was past all this now and considered himself fiscally responsible. What did I know? Managing the little money I acquired required a language and set of skills I was not conversant with. But let's get back to one of the pleasures of choice here, quality cigars. We all loved our Cubans convinced they were the best in the world bar none. Smoking was illegal in public places. Dirt didn't care, but as a minor concession to what he called "public indecency" did instill a whisper quiet and highly effective vent system in the bar area. The place was never blue cloud smoky and the dining area was free of smoke. Neither did the town officials. The few complaints, always placed by snooty tourists who thought they were God's gift to the planet, were dismissed in court for all sorts of reasons – lack of witnesses, lassitude, failure of complainants to appear and the fact that Ray's was good for the town's economy. The tourists were also a gift and spent their dough mad or not, something along the lines of a fool and his money are soon parted, but I'm digressing again and it's not the whiskey, I hope.

I was seated on my usual stool at the end of the bar where I could look out the window at passing trains, traffic and the weather. At the end of a hard day either working my Ed Bouchee Private Investigations gig – infidelity and check kitting are us - or writing weird stories about fly fishing for some magazines that I'd sold stuff to for years, even a couple of published novels that may have sold upwards of 800 copies combined, I would wander the two blocks up to Ray's with The Dog to have a few. I rarely worked hard but felt that I deserved this reward anyway. The Dog, a black on white five year old Springer, was asleep on a wooden bench beneath the window curled up on a quilt Dirt's grandmother had made long ago at the family homestead in the Pacific Northwest. The quilt was beautiful, an heirloom and worth lots of money. Nothing was too good for The Dog. The grey haired, sometimes slightly stooped owner (bad back from painting day after day) hauled the masterpiece, that was stored in a small cedar chest, into the bar one afternoon expressly for the animal. He spread the quilt over the bench's seat with a grand flourish and under the Springer's critical eye fine-tuned the arrangement. The Dog hopped, circled counterclockwise several times, collapsed with a satisfied "hrmph" and fell asleep. Successes on small levels are uncommon, beautiful creations to be savored and wondered at as they softly glow in the often dim light of life's passing. This kindness to my canine companion was no exception. The Dog and Dirt were close. Real close. Whenever anyone complained, tourists always the noisome culprits, about The Dog's presence in the bar Dirt would say, "You have two choices Sport, buy that dog a plate of deep-fried calamari or leave." Most bought my companion the squid, a dish the hound loved. The few that left rarely filed a complaint and the few that actually did follow through with their legal threats went away like the cigar complaints – up in the smoke of civil apathy.

The Dog got his name when one windy day (it blows a lot around here as weather pours down off of the Yellowstone caldera 50 miles south and sweeps through the Paradise Valley and blasts the town with gusts over 90 mph with some frequency) after a year of him refusing to acknowledge any of the names I tried to give him – Bonzo, Rupert, Zack, Ernie Banks. Without a thought I referred to him by his now accepted name when a potential client asked his name. I said "The Dog" for the hell of it and the little guy jumped off the couch where he liked to sleep and watch TV, bounded onto my lap and gave me a look that seemed to say "Finally you got it right, buddy." I could only figure that he'd been watching a rerun of the interview on Palladia with U2 guitarist The Edge. The Dog was easily influenced by television programming, most lately Blue Mountain dog food commercials. That's all he would eat now. So here's The Edge, whose guitar playing The Dog liked (he has all of the band's CDs courtesy of me and Amazon), holding forth about melody and minor key chords on this "legends" show and that's how history in Biederbeck style was made. The Edge. The Dog. Actually made a bit of sense to me. Dirt often said "That dog is a lot smarter than you. He knows things you'll never know." I suppose he's right even though I'm convinced that the cheese slipped off Dirt's cracker a long time ago. He's one of the best, but like the rest of us, mad as a hatter.

I was working on my first highball glass (ordered half full for the illusory sake of moderation) of Jim Beam (the booze of better slammers everywhere not Jack Daniels as the movies try and make you believe, the fools) and slowly working away on a Partagas Series E No.2 when Dirt walked up and leaned across the bar.

"What'd you think of those three developers being shot

up yesterday? Won't miss 'em. Greedy bastards are bad for the state. Still, a messy way to go. Bodies and raft shot to hell, shredded. That's what Qualls told me this morning over at the Post Office. He said that the sight will stick with him forever. That it was enough to make him regret being Sheriff. Don't blame. Gutting an antelope makes me queasy. Whoever did this must have used something high powered like a Mac-10 or Uzi. Hope their blood didn't make the trout sick." Dirt could be such a caring soul at times.

"From what I heard the killer slaughtered them with hundreds of rounds, like some drive by East LA drug hit," I said. "Things are going to hell everywhere. "

Following the discovery of the grizzly aftermath of an unknown assassin by a drift boat of anglers later that afternoon who were working a bankside run that fed into the logjam where the submerged remains of the three men in question and the mangled raft remained, local and state cops had been all over the place questioning anyone who knew or knew of the men. My response was that I'd seen them around town and on the river, from the distance of the opposite shore, over the last year, but that's as far as it went. Saw them here in the bar, but wasn't impressed by their loud, big mouth BS, so I ignored them. It seemed that nobody around town knew anything more than I did or at least that's the story they were sticking with. A couple of FBI agents from Butte 100 or so miles west of here were doing forensics on the bodies and Avon raft hoping to gather some clues about the slaughter – fingerprints, DNA, bullet caliber ID - the usual slick stuff that more often than not leads nowhere, despite what you see on those glitz investigative shows. They'd been called, well the FBI national office had been contacted by the state boys because the crime may have involved the Interstate Highway system and state lines may have been crossed. What the Highway Patrol really wanted was the FBI's forensic crime lab involvement in the matter. If a few jurisdictional toes got stepped on in the process, too bad. The pair of agents at the site comprised the Butte's entire staff. The bureau had downsized and thought of closing, still did from year to year, the office located not far from the edge of the Berkeley Pit, an enormous hole gouged out of the ground starting in 1955 with copper ore in mind. Why the Butte office was involved and not the Bozeman office made no sense to me. Perhaps this was a case of internecine politics, an internal agency squabble, not that this made any difference in solving the mess. Regardless, even lower tier FBI agents were damn good if not prone to rudeness, overbearing behavior and condescension, and the national crime lab was second to none in the world. The agency's involvement, though most likely contentious with other officers, could only help. Still, the lack of facts or witnesses to solve the case hinted that fast results and swift realizations didn't appear to be in the offing. I felt that this was going to be a tough case to crack.

"Beats me. I thought they were jerks of the first order. Big shot businessmen who trample anyone for a buck. Dime a dozen, top shelf assholes. Weird that there were no foot prints around the spot. Pretty dusty ground. And no shell casings. There must have been hundreds of rounds fired. Those two items bother me. Obviously someone was more than a little teed off with their act. Almost looks like a crime of passion, passion over what's right. Could be anybody – an angry rancher they screwed on a land deal, a less than satisfied client. They charge an arm and a leg for their services. Even when ranchers are happy they're in a surly mood, so I'd start with anyone outside of town they'd had dealings with. Then again it could have just as easily been some wandering wacko with some serious firepower, a guy who's probably already drinking his brains out down in Magdelena, New Mexico or some other wind-blown, dusty, end of the road, nowhere place. We get a few of these Bozos around here you know."

"I know. I see one or two in here every week trying to bum drinks off the respectable clientele such as The Count and yourself. Still, your take is how I see it," said Dirt as he poured me another drink. "No shell casings is odd unless another drift boat or raft overtook them and fired from the middle of the river and the ones that didn't land in the boat are now drifting along the bottom on their way to the Missouri. This happened far enough from the highway that it could easily have gone unnoticed. Distance, cottonwoods, tall grass, cut banks, all of these might make seeing the murders impossible from the interstate.

"I'd like to ask you a favor. Consider looking into this for me. I'm curious and have a hunch this is even more curious than it already seems. This might prove ugly for anyone who floats the river. I don't want to get blown away while I'm casting a Woolly Bugger to a brown trout on the river."

Let's be honest here. Dirt and I are not being cute or evasive when we refer to the Yellowstone as the river. That's what the locals call this outrageously gorgeous 525-mile ribbon of perfection. The river. That gets it.

"Not my style and more importantly, I don't see any money involved."

"Tell you what, Ed, you and The Dog nose around some and I'll clear your tab, and while working on this for me, all drinks, cigars and food are gratis. I'll even cover your gas expenses if that old rig still runs."

"What the hell's this "gratis" jive? I'm not into Latin."

"That's enough, Ed," said Dirt. He smiled and asked "What about it?"

"I don't even know the names of the dead guys."

"Lee Smith, Alan Trammell and Ted Klusewski. First two are from southern California. Klusewski hails from Texas, God love him. None of them has lived here more than six years and they're split residences at that."

"How do you know all this shit?

Dirt grinned his slight grin and walked down the bar to refresh the faithful's drinks.

I sipped the whiskey, puffed the cigar and considered the proposition. I was finished with my latest investigation, a case of marital infidelity that yielded a fair amount of acrimony for the frolicking couple and a few bucks for me. I'd just finished a short story on fly fishing for northern pike on the Blackfeet Reservation up near the Alberta border on a little creek that flowed right by an old abandoned and quite haunted radar base built during the embryonic beginnings of the Cold War and how all this influenced the outcome of the campaign of a public yahoo running for the US Senate. Ghosts and political hacks are a lot like cash under the table and city managers. The Flyfish Journal bought the thing and paid me hundreds of dollars, five hundred to be precise for the right to do so. How the two mixed together in the narrative surprised even me. I just write the stuff. I'm always grateful for any money anyone pays for my words and slightly addled thoughts. Factor in how my tab was cruising the rarified atmosphere of seven hundred dollars and Dirt's modest offer gained momentum. Besides, his hunches about things were a bit spooky and mostly on point, like the one about the illegal game poaching and bison slaying I investigated a while back. A stone cold murderer named Miskis was responsible. He's been dealt with, killed, and now all is well on that twisted front. And to make things really viable, my '83 Suburban, a recent acquisition, had new tires, a recent oil change and a tune-up. Pal, the GMC was tan and light brown sort of like a Palomino horse, was ready to go, all 14 mpg of her.

"Hoopy toopy ten four. Why not," I said finishing my drink. "I'll get on it tomorrow, but I'm staying well out of the cops' way."

"Good man. I'll come with you for some of this. Love a good mystery and we'll sneak some fishing in on the side." said Dirt. He poured another Beam for me, this time glass full. Done deal.

***

The drive to the murder site was about 20 miles or 15 minutes on I90, the four lane highway was busy handling semis, ranchers in expensive pickups, gargantuan motorhomes with plates from all over the place – Alaska, Florida, Illinois, even Hawaii. I couldn't figure the last one. How did the 50-feet of over-priced junk cross the Pacific? Did it raise a sail and float to Los Angeles harbor? Tourist season was moving along nicely except in Yellowstone Park where gridlocked roads and macadam campgrounds offered all the wilderness charm of an inner city say the aforementioned LA. It was another beautiful day in Montana. High summer is magic, almost as spectacular as September and October. A few fluffy clouds, temperature in the low nineties. Near zero humidity – nine percent today, with a light breeze out of the southwest bordered on meteorological perfection. The river rolled on in natural contrast with the road's artifice, a serpentine companion. Despite the volume of traffic, no one had seen or heard anything - not the murder, not any suspects, not a getaway car or truck. Even on busy days there were often gaps in the traffic of several miles and minutes. The killing might have happened during one of these stretches. The river swirled, raced and splashed sapphire beneath large cottonwoods, over gravel bars and through narrowing channels where rock cliffs squeezed the flow. Standing waves, small whirlpools and fast moving slicks made this stretch interesting from a floating perspective.

Hasil Adkins was growling something about no more hotdogs on the Suburban's CD player. This was The Dog's latest musical flame. He'd been lying on the couch in the

13

office while a documentary on the guy played on some obscure cable channel. Maybe it was the Food Channel. Hasil had lived a strange life and apparently wasn't too popular with his West Virginia mountain neighbors, The Haze as he called himself had three loves in life "girls, guitars and cars." After a series of run-ins with the law – living with an underage girl, a shootout with a jealous husband, illegal possession of a shotgun - he was done in when a teenager on an ATV nailed him in his front yard. His music is often described as rockabilly but after listening to his stuff on the sound track for White Lightnin' (a profoundly twisted movie that I've watched a number of times. Do your own math here) I'd say his genre was more like "devil-worship-abilly." Hasil was the real deal not some examining one's emotional navel divas like The Backstreet Boys or even that literary giant Rick Dolomieu.

Two days had passed since the murders now called The River Slaughters" by the media. Reports aired on every newscast including the national outfits like CNN, Fox and MSNBC. I was waiting to see how Rachel Maddow would manage to spin this atrocity into a hate crime against some maligned politically correct segment of our society. I had faith in the old girl. She'd pull this off with her accustomed pedantic aplomb replete with smirks, bizarre voice intonations that called to mind spring cattle branding, and the raising of eyebrows in ways that defied accepted physics. I couldn't wait. But I always was well aware of the fact that the story as national news had the shelf life of a goose fart on a muggy day. Attention span of gerbils and all that. Give me fresh meat not yesterday's horrific produce.

None of the many travelers along I90 had seen anything. Not the murder. Not the perps – I love cop talk. Not a vehicle near the crime scene even though a rough and dusty dirt road ran alongside the river mimicking its more impressive four-lane paved cousin soaring 30 feet along the raised roadbed nearby. No one had driven it since the last rain a month ago according to experts who looked closely at this. The East-West rail line also dogged the river. Nothing reported by any train crews. Several people did report a biplane that they described as yellow or maybe yellow and blue swooping low over the river and adjacent hail fields. A few phone calls quickly chalked this up to John Lester, a 60 year old rancher, who was weathered red-brown from decades of sun and wind. He stood six feet two inches and weighed, maybe, 200 pounds. The last time I saw him he was tossing metal fence stacks in the back of the truck, heavy loads, like he was loading small sacks of groceries. The guy was fit, strong, tough as nails as they say. He lived in near complete isolation in the sere, desiccated emptiness around the Cayuse Hills about 20-25 miles north of the murders. The family spread that began as a modest homestead in the 1880s was now over 200 sections or about 200 square miles or 130,000 acres, a large ranch where Lester managed to run about 600 head of Angus and a couple of dozen Pinzgauer, a breed native to Salzburg, Austria. The animals' meat made well-marbled superb rib eye steaks that state restaurants paid lots of money for whenever one of the one-ton cows was butchered. Best steaks I'd ever eaten. Antelope and mule deer along with turkeys, ruffed and sage grouse ran all over the place. A couple of spring creeks reportedly held enormous Yellowstone cutthroat trout and some cold water ponds played host to huge largemouth bass. Way out here when you wanted wild game you went out and shot it and to hell with official game hunting seasons. One hell of a place he had going way out there far away from anybody. I envied his good fortune.

Aside from raising cattle, shooting antelope, mule deer and game birds in the fall, well I'd guess mostly in the fall. I doubted state game wardens kept a real close eye on the man, Lester augmented his income. He'd once been quoted in Biederbeck's renowned daily newspaper, The O'Keefe County Standard, that called itself a daily newspaper if Saturday and Sunday didn't count, as saying his income was piss poor and that there wasn't any money to be made in "Chasn' cows back through fences they've just run down. If they were to make a movie of my f**k*d up life it would be 90 minutes of some hapless bastard running after his brain-dead cows swearing like a crazy fool, which he clearly must be to live like this. The closing shot would be of this idiot, and yes, that would be me, drinking whiskey and mending fence. Hell, I'd pay to see that. Wouldn't you?" That was John Lester in a nutshell, though he was nobody's fool. He had degrees in agriculture and engineering from Montana State University over in Bozeman. And I'd heard he had a library of rare books numbering in the thousands, lots of vinyl recordings and even more DVD movies. Lester was no trouble to anyone in these parts except maybe himself. Like a lot of us he was opinionated to the extreme and loved his whiskey. From personal experience I can vouch for the pleasantness of this combination. People, especially women, love the hell out of a drunken loudmouth drunk who thinks he knows everything about everything. The fact that I did failed to ameliorate this obnoxious behavior. He'd been contracted by another rancher, Ted Abernathy, to spray his enormous canola fields over by a little hamlet named Springdale. Senior hipsters and possibly a few felons called the place home. Police calls to both men confirmed this. Lester began the spraying last Monday morning, two days before the rampage on the river. Abernathy faxed the contract for the spraying to Qualls at the sheriff's office. A dead end that never looked good to begin with. If you were to ask Lester he'd probably say "Just like my damned life."

I took a ranch access exit off I90 and pulled around

through a short tunnel that lead to the dirt road by the murder site. After bouncing over the train tracks, we drove a mile downstream and away from the interstate, the sound of traffic muted by three-quarters of a mile distance and the sounds of the rushing water and wind. We were stopped by a state trooper who said we couldn't go any farther. He was stern and a bit surly, probably from the sun and heat and perhaps bored after the initial rush of excitement two days ago. Cop cars, cop pickups and a Montana Dept. Fish, Wildlife and Parks helicopter dominated the scene, red, blue and white lights were flashing all over the place despite the fact that the crime was almost 48 hours old - Barney Fife at full tilt on the Montana plains. I turned around and drove back a few hundred yards parking in the shade of some cottonwoods on the highway side of the tracks. I told The Dog to stay in the rig, put in Hasil's *What Was I Thinking* CD and struck for a large, exposed gravel bar 200 yards below all the cops. My friend understood and preferred shade to hot sun anyway. He curled up and was snoring in seconds. How anyone could sleep through Hasil was beyond me. Shrugging my shoulders I headed off clutching my Zeiss binoculars, a pocket digital camera jammed in my hip pocket. Short walk. Hot sun. After skulking along the tracks for a while I slid and stumbled a dozen feet down the loose dirt cut bank to the gravel bar and then worked my way across the gravel and rock to the edge of the river. I bent over and splashed water on my face, then soaked my 1938 Cubs replica ball cap and pulled it back on. The moist cold felt just fine. 1938 was the year the Yankees swept them 4-0 in the Series. Such is life.

I scanned the logjam where the raft and bodies were discovered by the passing fishermen. County, state cops and a pair of guys wearing dark blue windbreakers, despite the heat, with bright yellow FBI plastered on the backs and matching ball caps. Tweedle Dee and Tweedle Dum. Both men about six-feet or a little more and 185 pounds or a little less. Dark brown hair and matching outdoor walking shoes. A couple of real beauties. I loved the FBI.

"Hoop-toopy, ten-four."

Not much left to see. The body and raft parts were now at the state crime lab and state coroner's lab over in Helena, the state capital about 150 miles west, northwest of here. There was lots of yellow crime scene tape like you see on all the police shows shuddered in the wind, and that was it except for law enforcement trying to look busy or saying the hell with that and puffing on cigarettes while shooting the breeze.

This was pointless, but I'd tried. I started scoping the water to see if I could spot any dark shadows of holding trout or caddisflies being blown off the water. The powerfully sharp Zeiss lenses pulled me into the river – fish, bugs, a sculpin minnow sliding streambed tight from one dark spot to the next, some lime colored moss swirling in the current and a bunch of bright brassy cylindrical objects. What the hell? I looked again. Bullet casings? Maybe. The crime scene is over two football fields upriver. No gun expels shell casings that far even in a downwind, full on gale. I set the camera and binoculars on a large, flat rock and waded out knee deep into the river. The water was cool, not cold. I stooped down and reached up to mid bicep to snare what I now saw was a spent shell casing. I grabbed another. There were some markings on the backs around the pinged primer. I could make out 7.65x53 on top and PPU on the bottom of both - Prvi Partizan ammo from Uzice, Serbia. I knew the stuff. Don't ask me how I know this. Remember the riff about everything about everything? It's tough being the only sane man on the planet. The cartridges aren't rare but not all that common either. I spotted a half-dozen or more casings in deeper and faster water. I shoved my two into a pants pocket - concealing and withholding evidence without a care out here on the northern high plains. I started back to the Suburban.

The two FBI agents were leaning against the front of my rig, arms crossed, stern expressions made real scary with the wrap around black shades - real tough guys. This wasn't good. I was in big trouble. I hope I didn't have to stay after school and copy pages from a dictionary. That would be awful. I've had contact with agents from the FBI over the years. Most of them were tough, taciturn and guys who looked like they'd seen their share rough of doings. This pair resembled milquetoast, cardboard cutout versions of the real thing. I took this as an indication that the agency had bigger fish to fry. I love skillful use of metaphor but this will have to do. Like the posse comitatus goofballs in the northeast corner of the state. Bloody, flesh shredding butchery was commonplace these days, work for the lesser outfits in the law enforcement chain of significance. Apparently the state cops and Qualls, and most likely in the end Qualls and his officers would be solving this on their own.

"We know who you are Bouchee," one said. "Some small town PI pain in the ass who's mission in life seems to be getting in the way of law enforcement or working on two-bit divorce cases."

"How kind of you to notice," I said. "Who's watching the store back in Butte? Your aunt?

"Right at this moment you need to tell us what you're doing here, not straining your brain trying to be clever." the other asked.

"I got tired of playing NHL 14 on my computer, so I decided to take a look at the murder site like the other three million people that already have done the same thing. I'm not breaking any laws or violating the crime scene."

"You're a useless smartass." I think this was Tweedle Dee. "And who plays video games on a PC. Get a Game Boy, dipshit."

"How kind of you to notice. Thanks for tipping me to Game Boy. You FBI boys are really up on the high tech stuff. I can see that. I'm impressed."

The other agent moved towards me. He looked more pissed off than the other one. His buddy followed his lead. I was going to jail. I could see it. I worried about The Dog.

Life can have its fortuitous moments even for derelicts such as myself. Sheriff Jim Qualls pulled up in cloud of dust, leaped from his country pickup and came to my rescue.

"What's Ed done now?

The FBI couple looked at each other and one of them came up with, "He's been disrespectful." The other nodded in agreement. A couple of bright bulbs here. No wonder Washington wanted to shitcan the Butte office.

"To paraphrase that television crime show legend Detective Joe Kenda 'If being disrespectful is a crime, we should put up a tall fence around Biederbeck and tell all the residents that they're under arrest.'"

Tweedle Dum, I think, looked confused but did manage to come up with "Is everyone a wise ass around here?" looking at Qualls as he did so. Snappy rejoinders bounding about in the Montana summer air.

"Hey. They gave me grief for not having a Game Boy. I don't have to take that crap."

Qualls looked off down river, did a quick ten count and said, "I'll handle Ed. Go back to what you were doing."

The two held their ground for a few seconds, an FBI pride thing I imagine, then they walked, no make that strode back to the yellow tape and down to the river.

"What the hell are you doing here, Ed? And what's this Game Boy stuff."

"Nosing around. I'm curious. I think you might tell those two to go down and look in the water just off that gravel bar," I said while pointing to where I'd just been. "A bunch of brass out there. Don't ask about the Game Boy. It just came up in passing"

Qualls and I were long-time friends. He looked at me then again away, this time to the Beartooths off in the southern distance. I was sure he'd rather be above 10,000 feet fishing some lonesome, spectacular mountain cirque for golden trout than dealing with me.

"Thanks for cooling out those two. I really was keeping to myself. I even kept The Dog in the Suburban."

"Makes me proud to be your friend," said Qualls. "Of course you didn't grab a couple of those shells for yourself, did you?" Qualls' expression indicated that he was confident that I'd done just that.

"No way. Not me," I said looking as innocent as I was capable, an expression that in most states was at the very least a tacit admission of guilt.

"Okay. After you leave, like right away, I'll tell those two what you saw."

"Some damn big cutthroat nymphing in the corner pocket a little above the bar. You might want to rake a few casts. They're there to be had."

"Ed." Qualls stopped, looked at me, smiled and walked towards the FBI boys. "See you at Rays later on," he said over his shoulder.

"I'll be there."

"There's one big dandy of a surprise."

Qualls dropped down to the river near the logjam. I climbed in the GMC, started the engine, and headed for town. I put the Doors *Strange Days* on the player. This seemed appropriate. The Dog, after looking me over, went back to sleep, too tired to fly his big floppy ears in the jet stream out the window as I motored down the highway at 80 mph.

***

The next morning was more of the same weather wise

– a few clouds, blue sky, breeze already up and heat on the way. That's how it would be until the August Singularity, a predictable cold, wet weather system that always showed up around the 23rd of that month for a day or two. Then warm and clear again, but not hot anymore, as the days shortened and cooled off until the rains then snows of late October and November held sway.

Over drinks and dinner at Ray's with Qualls, we ate at the bar – burgers for Jim and I, calamari for The Dog, he told me that there were no leads. Not a one. Cell phones had been recovered but were in bad shape, maybe nothing useful due to their battered condition, computers confiscated and now being analyzed, relatives informed and questioned, past histories run, but nothing so far. There were three individuals who apparently fancied themselves fly fishing hipsters dressing like fifties jazz players replete with white shirts, skinny black ties, black trousers and pork pie hats, the attire worn even while floating the river, that were questioned. Their alibi was that they'd been playing music and had not been on the river was confirmed when a local recording studio owner, Dexter Fowler, stated that they'd been recording various versions of *It Ain't Necessarily So* from 6 a.m. through 8 p.m. on the day of the murders. I'd seen the curious trio a number times on the river in their eccentric garb. The boys could cast and often were playing a large trout when I floated by. I wondered if they wore wading boots or wingtips. The scent of reefers burning in the air was ever-present and they seemed to like Pabst Long-necked beer. I never got close enough to find out any of the details. We always give each other slight nods. They were okay in my book and no way could they have done this. Doubt they had the capabilities to even imagine such a scenario. Angling hipsters on the loose in Montana. You had to live here for a while to appreciate some of this. Other than this, Qualls had little to report. He was waiting on various lab results, though from what he'd seen and been told, not much would be forthcoming on this front. A high-profile set of murders that looked like it had real chance of going unsolved. What with the Freemen acting up again in the last week over in Jordan, a really small wind swept, dusty berg right out of High Plains Drifter, proclaiming their support for the inbred subnormal Bundy rancher clan, avoiding a major bullet-filled conflagration had most law enforcement's attention these days. We talked some more and then went our separate ways.

***

I'd called Lester last night from Ray's and asked if he'd be up for a visit. He said "Why not?" No way did I think he was involved, but maybe he'd seen something while dusting Abernathy's fields. It was worth a shot and maybe I could squeeze in a little fishing on Lester's place.

Despite being a certified loner, his home was always open to those he knew. We'd been casual friends for years sharing drinks at Rays, running in to each other at the hardware, liquor or grocery store or several times at the tire dealer where it seemed that whenever I bought a new set of Cooper's he was there buying Toyos for one of his pickups. We shared common interests like fly fishing, upland bird hunting and the love of good country. Lester owned a lot of that. I'd been fortunate to be invited to fish his bass ponds a couple of times. Large, powerful fish, eager to take any large fly. His spring creeks were a bit different. The icy, clear flows held large trout, but they were selective, discerning, preferring small flies and cautious casts. Never fished those, yet. All this was nestled in the middle of spectacular surroundings. The ice-scoured valleys of the Norton's cut their way up to snow covered peaks above 10,000 feet off to the west. Both the Abasaroka and Beartooth Ranges stood to the south and on really clear days from a tall bluff not far from his home you could just make out the Big Snowy

Mountains way up by Lewistown 100 miles north - more towering illusion than solid reality. Beneath all of these ranges the land rolled off forever in large ochre, tan, salmon, charcoal and light grey hills, bluffs, mesas and plateaus roughly cut with coulees weathered rough and near impassable from thousands of years of rain and choked with dead clumps of Russian thistle, cactus and chokecherry brush. A few rattlesnakes too. Native grasses moved on the land like an ocean standing place. Antelope bucks with 15-16-inch horns reclined in the sun on slopes above their harems grazing below them. Some of the largest elk anywhere held in those deep coulees only coming out near dark or during heavy overcast or after summer night thunderstorms that pounded the land with hundreds of strikes per minute along with high wind, torrential rain and hail. I'd been trapped out in the open during a few of these. They were terrifying, life changing experiences. The elk here dwarfed those I'd seen elsewhere except for a few tucked away deep in the Missouri Breaks well north of Lewistown. Waterfowl used the ponds and spring creeks as rest stops on their migrations north in the spring and south in autumn. Sandhill cranes, enormous birds standing several feet tall, fed by the thousands in Lester's freshly-turned fields each April - avian dinosaurs clacking away day and night in an ancient roar. Mule deer wandered the land as did lots of Sage grouse, sharp-tailed grouse, turkeys and a few pheasants. To my eyes the place was unreal, heaven on earth.

Lester didn't ask why I wanted to visit. He didn't seem to care.

"Bring a rod, a small one – 6-6 or seven feet. The rainbows and cuts are busy in the creeks taking mayflies. Small ones." He said. "Here's a real surprise for ya'. I'll be fixing fence about a mile from the main barn. Follow the gates and leave them as you find them whether they be opened or closed. The two-track isn't much, but you'll make if you watch for the ruts cut and dried in the gumbo from the spring rains."

We chatted a bit, but not about the murders on the river before hanging up. I picked up a couple of bottles of R&R Reserve, Lester's favorite booze, and put a half dozen H. Upmann Magnum 46 cigars, vintage 2005, in a zip lock bag. I'd bought several hundred a couple of years back and still had about half the lot. He liked these always saying "Best damn cigar I ever smoked." I left The Dog home. He wouldn't bother Lester's cows, but I wanted to make things as smooth and easy as possible for this visit. Dirt said he'd check in and feed and water him late in the afternoon.

The drive took me past the crime scene, now abandoned. The FBI and state boys left town last night, leaving the local cops to muddle along while they examined the evidence they'd gathered. There was a lot – body and raft parts and maybe even a few shiny brass shell casings. One never knew. Analysis would take weeks. Since there'd been no quick arrest and attendant hero stories normally, the FBI and state cops moved off to work on the next horror while lab technicians and coroners did their work on the river massacre. Qualls and his deputies would stay on the case talking to anyone they received a tip on or anyone who looked like questioning might yield some curiosity related to this madness. All the law enforcement agencies would stay on the case, each in their own way, using their own methods and at their own pace. Yellow crime scene tape still fluttered in the breeze now turned into a hot wind and it was not yet 10 am. At Stillwater I turned north on 191 and drove the narrow two-lane highway that was dangerous as hell, even in good weather. Trucks passing on hills and blind corners, wide loads of hay and passing game and range cattle provided enough excitement to keep me focused on the task at hand.

The Norton's seemed to come closer and then drift back into the distance as the road wound back and forth and up and down steep valleys that held small creeks that stayed moist with the helping hand of cold springs that perked up all over the place, even amidst stretches of sage, cactus and dusty white saline seeps. After 40 focused miles of driving I spotted Lester's large, rusting, metal mailbox. He'd painted his name on it - LESTER. The metal gate was open. That was it. He didn't need any Ponderosa type log entrance to mark the turn in. The man knew where he lived. I angled right off 191 heading east on a good gravel road for the seven mile drive to his house.

The slow drive in wasn't much, just a world filled with wild, serene splendor and nothing else. The fact that all of this still existed was almost enough for me, a lot like driving for hundreds of miles, hour after hour through the dense green and secretive still, dark waters of the boreal forest in the Northwest Territories on my way to Great Slave Lake. There was freedom in all this. Low grade anxiety, fear, anger, manic behavior no longer existed.

Pulling into the big turn around and grassy dirt yard at Lester's place felt like coming home for some reason. His truck, an older red 1978 Dodge Power Wagon was gone. The homestead residence had grown over the decades into a rambling structure with one and two-story additions. The place was now over 4,000 square feet. A lot of space for one man to make feel like home. A feeling of emptiness, aloneness emanated from the rambling home. On a gate near the barn and sheds a cardboard sign was ducked taped. Thru Hear it said in black dry marker. Hear? Lester joking a little, maybe? I pulled up, opened the gate, went "Thru Hear," stopped and closed the gate. Angus grazed and stood statue still far down a small, grassy crease in the land. Ten minutes of lurching and the Suburban being flung side to side by the deep ruts in the two-track brought me to Lester's truck, impeccably maintained but showing the wear from decades of work, fence posts and tools scattered across the tailgate and in the bed. He was a few yards away crimping some wire dressed in faded jeans, chambray work shirt, worn work boots and a Stetson hat marked with a dark band of sweat. The hat was creased, battered and worn. An item for cheating the sun and the rain, not a phony showoff item. In his sixties, Lester looked fit, lean and could go all day. When he finished, he took off his hat, wiped his brow and said in a strong, deep voice that held the land's timeless resonance in it, "Good to see ya, Ed. I'm near done."

I grabbed my leather work gloves that I always have on the front seat for changing flats and helped him finish the work. Then we went back to our rigs. I pulled a couple of beers out of a cooler full of ice and grabbed the two bottles of R&R, and the bag of cigars. I put the booze and four of the smokes on the bench seat of Lester's Dodge before handing him a beer and an Upmann 46. He watched me do all of this, simple acts that turned out to be more of a juggling act than I'd anticipated. He smiled, a crease that brightened his face like sunlight on still water. After we opened the cans, cut and lit our cigars, savored a few gulps of beer and draughts of smoke, Lester turned and looked me over with the appraising perusal of a veteran cattle buyer, which indeed he was. Here was a man who could assess what he saw and make quick, accurate judgments.

"You're alright, Ed," he said, deep blue eyes sparking in the light. "Nothing wrong with Pabst. Dad drank a lot of it when he went to college back in Wisconsin at UW in Madison. Got his engineering degree there, near the top of his class. Full scholarship 'cause he could carry a football. Tough SOB that way.

"Pabst is good beer and a fair price, at least for these times. What kind of fool pays eight bucks for a six pack of something called Moose Drool? Sometimes I think our species is doomed."

He drew on the cigar and said "Still the best damn cigar I ever smoked."

I agreed and we shot the breeze about cattle prices – they were up slightly, bird populations, and his spring creeks. Fly fishing was as much a part of my life as anything. I couldn't restrain myself.

"It's okay Ed. I understand. Get that way when I think about all sorts of things like flushing sharptails on a pretty October afternoon. Stirs the blood and feels real romantic in a high plains way. We'll get to those trout soon enough. Hope you brought the right length rod."

"I brought two, a Heddon 6-6 Featherweight and a seven foot Orvis Deluxe Battenkill and a couple of Hardy Perfect reels."

Again the appraisal then the laugh I liked and would never forget. An honest sound like a fire cracking late into the evening while a sky full of stars, planets and meteors played its eternal tune. This was a good man who'd lived through a lot.

"Other than fishing and blabbing with me did you have a reason for coming on up?" he asked. No rancor or concern or suspicion. Lester was always up front. What you saw is what you got. I liked this in people. I'd much rather be told I was acting like a jerk than go on for hours pretending everything was Jim Dandy. Cut the jive and stay on point. This saved a lot of wasted and largely useless emotions like the hurt that invariably leads to anger or worse, the loss of a friend. I don't think about this silly shit much, but it's there in my head running its own cerebral railroad all the time.

"I heard you were spraying Ted's fields over Springdale way the afternoon of the murders and I wondered if you'd seen anything different or out of place."

More beer and smoke. A little time passed

"A state trooper and then one of those boys from the FBI asked me the same thing yesterday. Cops one after the other. I said the only unusual thing I saw was a fat buck white tail my plane spooked trying to leap a wood fence. Caught his big belly, then hind legs on the top rail and did a face plant in the grass. The big boy jumped right up and looked around probably to see if anyone had noticed his fuck up. Then he ran into the alder and willow along an old irrigation ditch. Nothing else. Where those men were killed was a couple of air miles away. It would have been tough to make out a killer or even his truck while I was bouncing around in the air. Can't hear a damn thing cause of the Grumman's engine noise. That 300hp Jacobs R-755 has a lot of power, but it's a loud son-of-a-bitch.

"Last time I was in the Nightowl, a day or two before the killings, those three and another guy were talking about what big shots they were, loud enough for the whole bar to hear. They also mentioned that they'd be floating the river and planned to take out at the Springdale Access. After two whiskey ditches I'd had enough and walked out. I told the cops that, too."

I went and pulled out two more beers. The cigars still had a long way to go. We were good on that front.

"That's what I figured. Dirt asked me to look into the murders as a favor. He's curious like always. Said he'd clear my bar tab."

"I imagine that's no small deal," said Lester. Again the casual but deep appraisal. "Dirt's a good guy. Need to stop in there for a meal soon."

"I'd have done this for free. Dirt's one hell of a good friend and I'm curious, too," I said. "I thought if anyone had noticed something out of the ordinary that day, it would have been you. And, hell, I wanted a crack at your spring creeks."

"That's how I figured your trip up this way," he said.

"No problem. We'll chase those trout when the sun drops some and the bugs start comin' off. 'Til then, let's head back. I'll grill some rib eyes I saved from an ornery Pinzgauer I butchered last month. Damn thing kept busting up my fences. Made good money on the beef. Sold it to that meat locker outfit in Butte. Cut down on the fence work some too. A good deal all around, except for the cow I imagine.

"No harm in sipping a little of that whiskey while we wait to eat and fish," the rancher said. "We'll make a night of it. You can stay in the guest room. You'll do fine there. Refrigerator. Bathroom. TV. A veritable fucking Holiday Inn Express."

"Man, that sounds good," I said. "I love it out here."

"I can see that."

We each drove back to the ranch house. What a beautiful day. Literally heaven on earth.

The steaks were fantastic. The whiskey was more than good. After we cleaned up, I rigged a rod, Lester said he'd watch or borrow the rod if need be. We crossed a barbed wire fence and walked along a level piece of land cleared of rocks and brush, a runway. The yellow Grumman was tied down inside a large aluminum hanger, sliding doors pushed full open, the space inside allowed the plane ample room. I could see a fuel tank, maybe a one-thousand gallon job, on a frame above ground, just outside the hanger. Tool boxes, oil drums and a workbench ran along one wall,

"Love that sucker. She's a real blast to fly and one of a kind. I got the flying bug from Dad. He loved vintage aircraft. He restored the Grumman and a few others. He could fix anything mechanically. I got the gene and can do the same. He sold off the others when times were lean, but hung on to the AgCat 'cause he could make money dusting with it. It's been part of this place for fifty years. Can't imagine life without it, knowing someone else is flying her. Silly, but that's how I feel. Dad learned to fly in World War

II. A nearby rancher flew a Nieuport 21 with the Lafayette Escadrille in World War One and then barnstormed. Guy's name was Harold "Bucky" Thaw. Bucky took a liking to Dad and taught him to fly. The Thaw place was bought up for back taxes by a group of California developers, maybe the same ones that got shot up, but that went nowhere, at least not yet. Waters sparse on that land as it can be here. I can track down the buyers' names if you want."

"Whenever you get the chance, I said. "It might lead to something."

"Dad enlisted in the Marines when the war broke out, with his engineering degree and flying experience he had little trouble getting what he wanted and that was being a pilot in the Pacific. Pearl Harbor made him hate the Japs. Friends of his were killed in that ambush. Flew F4U Corsairs. Shot down once, but he shot down four Jap Zeros during his tour out there and bombed the hell out of a lot of enemy soldiers. Mom died of cancer while he was gone. He came home a quiet, withdrawn man with a lot of sorrow and he stayed that way until he passed away from just being wore out and the stress of the war memories and Mom's dying, I think. That was in November 1980, a cold, snowy, windy day, shitty in the way only November can be – without color or life. The only close family I had left was my brother, Jim, who lived in Gardiner and worked in the Park. He died thirty years ago in September '96."

I didn't ask questions about any of this. We continued our walk to the creek in silence.

At the eastern end of the runway a small hill protruded from the dry surroundings. Two enormous wood plank doors marked an entrance into what appeared to be a mammoth earthen shelter. The wood was grey from the sun, wind and rain. They must have weighed a ton. A large shiny chain and padlock secured them. The metal sparkled in the waning light as the sun worked its way down behind the Nortons rising over 10,000 feet thirty miles away. Lester saw me looking at the place.

"Dad built that back in the seventies. He turned a small hole into a big one. Reinforced all of it with 12x12 timbers he got from a sawmill in Eureka in the northwest part of the state up above Whitefish. Used to be an entrance to an old mine that never yielded any gold to speak of. He must have worked on that place for a couple of years for God knows why. We already had a big barn and plenty of storage sheds. Now I park all my old machinery that's crapped out or been replaced by newer stuff. So full in there I can barely move around in there."

"How in the hell do you open those doors?" I asked.

"Ball bearing slide that is smooth as silk. One grunt and those babies slide right over. A little kid could open them," said Lester. "Keep telling myself I need to clean the place up, get rid of all the old machinery, but for some reasoning I can't bring myself to do it. Sentimental about Dad's old stuff, I guess. Haven't been in there in more than a year. Care to look inside?"

"That's okay, but thanks."

We walked the mile or so down a weathered cut in the land, eroded smooth by weather and time. The little creek was formed where a spring bubbled out of the ground a few hundred yards away out of a rock outcropping covered in emerald moss with thick bunches of grass guarding the water's source. The flow meandered for a couple miles before dumping into a larger stream that emptied into the Yellowstone many miles away. Watercress shoots moved lazily in the current like flags on a slow day. The streambed was sand and multi-colored rock that shone gem-like even in the low light, the water was that clear and the place seemed to have a light of its own. Natural magic I'd seen many times and at plenty of other places in Montana. As far as I'm concerned, when that light is all gone, the land is dead, killed by developers and the like. Hopefully I won't experience this in my lifetime. Trout were rising everywhere – big ones, little ones and all sizes in-between. They were brightly-colored Yellowstone cutthroat gliding through the water like gold ingots with all sorts of shades of red, pink and orange. Wonderful little fish. Those trout had made the long run up from the river centuries or more back along with some big browns every year in October and November to spawn according to Lester. For some reason mountain whitefish had not made an appearance in the spring creek, not a one, which was something of a mystery since they were common in the Yellowstone. Excited hands shook as I struggled to thread the slender leader tippet through the hook's eye.

"Settle down, Ed. The fish aren't goin' anywhere."

I finally tied the clinch knot to the small tan Humpy and made a cast about twenty feet upstream. The bunch of hair, thread and feathers tied to a little British-made hook settled on the water, drifted back to me a few feet before a fat trout sucked that up, raced and splashed around the stream before tiring. Eighteen inches, fat and gorgeous. By the time we'd finished admiring the trout and released it, the other cutthroat were back to feeding on the bugs. These guys weren't shy or easily spooked. Little if any fishing pressure was the key factor. More casts took more cutthroat and continued to do so until dark.

We kibitzed and laughed like the little kids we were at heart before I said that I'd had my fill, at least for now. Night came on, a crescent moon rose and we watched as a pair of huge elk the size of horses drifted up out of some secret spot deep in Lester's land and onto the prairie to feed.

Magnificent. Lester's land blew me away.

We drank a good deal of the R&R, smoked the four cigars I'd brought and talked away for hours about everything and nothing. Well past midnight we went to bed.

In the morning, Lester truck was gone. He was already off in some distant field, no doubt mending fence or some other never-ending chore.

A note written in pencil on a yellow legal pad set on the kitchen table by the coffee pot said, "Ed, Good time yesterday. You're welcome anytime. My place is yours. My two hired hands and I need to clear out a couple of irrigation ditches before they're totally plugged. Maybe I'll see you at Ray's this weekend. Thanks for the cigars and whiskey. One last thing, bring that goofy dog of yours along next time. I like that one. Maybe he can scare up some sharpies. Just about that time of the season. You can use my Darne 16 gauge if you like. John

I loaded up and reluctantly drove back to Biederbeck.

***

I was sitting in my office chatting with The Count, owner of a used appliance store. A tall man of eccentric and uncommon personality dimensions even by this place's standards and a good friend. Maybe the brightest guy in town, and despite the madness around here, that was saying a lot. Some of the smartest people I'd met in fifty-one years of living, called Biederbeck home. Were a lot of them crazy? Yes, but many of them were brilliant. The Count frequently wore Lederhosen, Tyrolean hat, white knee socks and Birkenstock sandals in summer, bushy white hair and mustache. You get the idea. Indeed a smart guy, but a freak like most of the rest of us in town, though Dirt and Qualls insisted that they were normal. They weren't fooling anyone. Those two were as goofy as the rest of us. Why this place of only a few thousand attracted so many creative misfits is a mystery. Windswept, dusty, sometimes very hot or very cold and surrounded by spectacular mountain ranges and the high plains and not much to hang its hat on trade wise except for cattle and the railroad, the town cruised along to its own beat. Hell, Biederbeck was often referred to as an asylum without walls by the straights living in other Montana burghs. I'd lived in the state since 1983 when I was eighteen. After spending a couple of years in the MFA creative writing program at the University of Montana in Missoula, I moved to Biederbeck for lots of reasons – a small town filled with members of the lunatic fringe like myself, the scenery, the river, the outstanding fishing and the more central location in Montana for way out there high plains adventures.

The Dog was asleep on the couch. He'd wake up around 4 p.m. and stare at me and the TV, back and forth until I turned on the Cubs-Pirates game. Jake Arrieta versus Ryan Vogelsong. Could be a good game. The TV was off. How he knew when something would be on that he wanted to watch, let alone knowing when a given program started was all beyond me. How do dogs know anything? I guess they just do.

We sipped beers, this time Special Export, formerly a fine beer, now an over-priced brew favored by the dot.com set, the vast minions of drone-like creatures plugged into "The boogey electric" as tenor sax man extraordinaire Rahsann Roland Kirk said way back when. Strohs was to blame for this one. The mega-brewer bought out the original maker, G. Heileman Brewing of LaCrosse, Wiaconsin. We all make mistakes. Eight bucks, but a friend from Presque Isle in the northern woods of the Badger state had shipped me four cases for my birthday last March. So I couldn't really complain too much. While talking away, The Count chain smoked his Camel Straights. I dealt with a cigar, flecks of ash all over my shirt. I'd asked my friend, who had been a spook during the latter stages of The Cold War for the CIA and stationed in Germany, which may have explained his garb, to look at the two 7.65mm casings I'd purloined from the scene of the murders.

Today was Thursday, July 30th, still hot, dry and ten

35

days out from the killings on July 20th, the day after a full moon. Go figure, just another lunatic slaying a day behind the lunar schedule. I expected to hear from Qualls any day now on the forensic examinations of the phones all retrieved in blasted bad shape and the confiscated computers of the three men – PCs, tablets, home machines. I wasn't anticipating anything earth shaking from the state coroner. I knew what had killed them, lots of the type of bullet the pair of casings on my desk represented. Hundreds it seemed. And mutilated remains are just that, mutilated remains.

The Count was holding forth on the shell casings. He'd been doing so for twenty minutes and showed no signs of letting up. The brass was now rolling around in his big right fist like a couple of deadly dice.

"The 7.65x53 Mauser cartridge was adopted by the Belgian military around 1889, so the 7.65x53 is commonly known as the 7.65 Belgian Mauser. Shortly thereafter the 7.65x53 was adopted by several South American countries, including Argentina, so it is also known as the 7.65mm Argentine, particularly in North America," he said between sips of Special Export that he'd poured in a ceramic, metal-lidded stein he always seemed to have with him. Mug in one hand, smoke in another The Count carried on.

"The 7.65x53 has a rim diameter of .474" and a case length of 53mm (2.09"). 7.65mm translates to .303 caliber in English usage, and the 7.65x53 uses the same .311" diameter bullets as the .303 British."

I tried to maintain contact with all of this by taking notes on a legal pad like the one Lester used only instead of a pencil, I used a Bic pen.

"Ballistically the 7.65x53 is similar to the .303 British cartridge. Handloaders should approach maximum loads with caution, as the old Mauser 1889/1890/1891 rifles in which the 7.65x53 is usually found are not as strong as the later Model 1898 Mauser or modern rifles. Factory loaded ammunition for the 7.65x53 (7.65mm Argentine) is available in this. Hand loaders do not have a great selection of .311 bullets, but it is adequate for most purposes - hunting big game, long range target shooting and apparently mangling fly fisherman on the river.

I tried to interrupt and ask a couple of questions, but no dice. The Count was on a roll, his deep voice rolling around the room and off the walls. The thousands of books and large Persian carpet I'd been given by my grandmother a long time ago – so many years, so many dear friends now gone, but the same ride for all of us - softened the sound somewhat. He hacked deeply on occasion and I worried about his health from all the cigarettes, but, hey, we're all big boys and can manage our own bad habits or we can't. The Count wasn't giving up his cigarettes and I wasn't quitting cigars as much to say "Up yours" to the PC Nazis as anything. Better dead than brain dead.

"According to the *Hornady Handbook, Third Edition* handloaders with Argentine Mausers in excellent condition or good commercial rifles can drive the 150 grain spire point bullet to a MV of 2400 fps with 36.1 grains of IMR 3031 powder, and 2700 fps with 41.1 grains of IMR 3031. The 174 grain Round Nose bullet can be driven to a MV of 2300 fps by 36.3 grains of IMR 3031 powder, and 2600 fps by 41.7 grains of IMR 3031. These Hornady loads were developed using Norma brass and Federal 210 primers in an 1891 Mauser rifle with a 29" barrel. And the Maxim gun, sometimes referred to by the uninformed as Spandau because so many were made in that Berlin bourough on the Havel River, can fire up to 500 rounds per minute.

"Because of the relative weakness of the early Mauser Model 1889, 1890, and 1891 bolt actions, the break-action combination guns are at least as strong and can handle pressures at least as high as those recommended for the rimless 7.65x53, so 7.63x53 rimless data should be safe to use for reloading the 7.65x53R cartridge."

He finished his beer and went over to the fridge for another. This was my chance.

"So finding the ammunition or even loading rounds yourself and also finding weapons to use with it would not be a problem?" I asked. The Count handed me a beer and settled into the red leather chair, an antique inherited from my step-father, parked on the Persian carpet on the other side of my desk. I'm a classy guy in an old-timey, haphazard way.

"Not at all. These two casings were made by Prvi Partizan in Serbia. You can see the PPU stamped on each one," said while holding the cartridges to me and pointing out the letters with a nicotine-stained index finger. He then placed them on the desk where they rolled into each other with a soft clink.

"Count, maybe all of the rounds came from a Maxim gun. It would explain a lot of things," I said. "What do you think?"

"It's possible, but not likely. Even the lighter air-cooled version weighs 26.5 kilos or 58.4 pounds and that's without a tripod or some other device to hold and steady the gun. The water cooled version weighs four kilos more. Certainly the perpetrator didn't hand hold the gun. Mounting one in the bed of a pickup is possible, but not that easy to accomplish, and would certainly stick out like a sore thumb going down the highway – the Rat Patrol Montana style. As intriguing as the thought might be, I seriously doubt that The Red Baron swooped down on these poor souls in a Fokker Dr.I triplane, those glorious days of civilized warfare are long gone, I'm afraid," The Count said and sighed into his beer blowing flecks of foam onto his moustache.

The office door swung open creating a blinding rectangle of sunlight, a mini cloud of dust and a blast of hot air my old air conditioner would be hard pressed to deal with. Qualls came in with it, all six-foot-three, 190 pounds of him. A high plains drifter in faded jeans, scuffed cowboy boots, a long-sleeved O'Keefe County Sheriff shirt with insignia – stitched in mountains, trees, river and the words "O'Keefe County Police, Protect and Service, and the obligatory sweat stained and weather worn Stetson. Qualls had been a star quarterback and state champion wrestler at O'Keefe High thirty years ago and was no man to cross. I'd watched as he dismantled tough-guy drunks 100 pounds heavier in a matter of seconds. A leather holster thread on his belt held a .45 Smith & Wesson ACP with a custom wood grip. The pistol held eight rounds plus one in the chamber. Qualls could hit what he aimed at, every time. In a smaller leather hold on his left hip was a Motorola two-way radio. A very high tech Motorola cellphone was wedged into his left shirt pocket. The machine would do damn near everything, but Qualls wasn't a robot constantly tied into and playing with the thing. It was a tool of the trade, nothing more. And he didn't carry mace or a Taser. The sheriff felt that these so-called non-lethal deterrents were too easy to use in the hands of a poor officer.

I carried a pistol, a S&W .357 that was either in my desk drawer, Suburban glove compartment or holstered to my belt along with a Buck hunting knife. If these two couldn't keep me out of trouble, I was doomed anyway.

My concession to living in the world of high tech madness was a six year old flip top cell phone and a police scanner bought at Radio Shack about the same time. Both the phone and scanner were usually turned off. Nothing all that important happened all that often in my life and the craziness and often horror spewing from the scanner drove me nuts. I'd managed to get by with these things on only a few hours each day, usually when I woke up around 5 a.m. until early afternoon. Email and USPS mail worked, too. My friends understood and cooperated with my archaic proclivities. A lot of us were dinosaurs around here and sadly, proud of it.

We were similar in many ways. Same build though he was in better shape. Same age. He had a little more hair. We both loved anything to do with the outdoors – fishing, bird hunting, camping. We both liked to drink, me more than him. We liked to read fiction and watch sports on TV and cherish our disdain for much of the superficiality passing itself off as thoughtful, caring living. And we'd both been divorced and never had experienced a great deal of good fortune with women.

He clocked the room and said "What a pair to draw to. The only sane one in here is that dog of yours."

"I assume that assessment includes you," said The Count.

Qualls laughed and parked his rear on an old dresser I'd scored at the local second hand store, Rod & Su's, for ten bucks. He declined a beer but helped himself to one of my Upmann 46s from the humidor at his right hip. I tossed him my lighter and he torched the cigar then flipped it back to me. I mishandled the relay and the lighter bounced on the old, battered desk that weighed a ton. Another knick added to the scarred wood surface. Soon clouds of blue-grey smoke from his cigar joined ours whirling around the ceiling fan like a diaphanous nebula.

"Got the results on the phones and computers along with the coroner's report," said the sheriff. "Death was caused by multiple, and I stress the word "multiple," gunshots apparently from 7.65x53mm shells, probably identical to those The Count's holding. A dozen rounds were recovered , but they're so degraded from impacts with flesh, raft material, water and rock, ballistics yielded little other than they went with the brass casings recovered at the crime scene. No tire tracks, boot tracks, foot prints, cigarette butts, nothing to show that anyone had been along that stretch of river for weeks. The whole thing feels like it took place in another time dimension Dental records and DNA confirmed the ID's of the dead men.

"The three victims – Lee Smith, Alan Trammell and Ted Klusewski – had clean records excepting a DUI or speeding ticket here and there," the sheriff said. "The only info on the computers and phones was work related or personal correspondence and websites – golf websites, cigar websites, fishing gear and the like, not even any porn on any of the devices. They were all involved in real estate deals, mainly closing on the Chiaco ranch up on Cottonwood Creek. Nothing else of real interest except some deal in Haiti involving flies being tied down there and shipped up here by way of Billings."

"I'm quite sure the three of us can all say the same about porn perusal," said The Count.

"Quite sure. We're all saints here" said Qualls. "All contacts on the phones and the computers, were interviewed from the perspectives of alibi, motive and opportunity. Despite making big bucks from real estate and fly fishing operations, they don't seem to have egregiously pissed off anyone, at least that we know of.

"One call came in to Trammell's phone while they were on the river, from Chuck "Twiggy" Hartenstein. Mainly chit chat about fishing and plans to meet for dinner later that day," Qualls continued. "Hartenstein was the fourth partner or cog in all the business dealings. The four had been friends for years. Gotten rich together and there is no sign of acrimony or shady behavior was turned up by either the FBI or Highway Patrol, unless you consider land development distasteful."

All of us despised the buying up old ranches often mutilating them by slicing the land into high-end, 20-30 ranchettes with homes all looking the same due to building covenants hustled to more out of state mooches with too much money for their own good. On one such holding, each home looked like a 20,000 square foot Ponderosa with only slight variations. I'd never find the right one after a few drinks at night if I lived there. These controlled, gated "communities" often had golf courses designed by the likes of Nicklaus, Palmer and Fazio. This seemed to be the way of the West these days. Look at Whitefish, Telluride, Sheridan, Wyoming and on and on - tragic but inevitable. Too many people on the planet. With apologies to rats, that's how our species now bred. The room was silent for a bit then The Count said, "Seems like this was nothing more, nothing less than a wicked drive-by executed by some sociopathic on killer steroids."

"That's more or less the operating premise right now and what with those wacked-out Freemen wannabes acting up again over by Jordan, official interest and spare manpower for our murders is next to nothing unless we turn up something substantial," said Qualls. We all worked on our smokes; The Count and I on our beers.

The door pushed open again. Biederbeck native Ron Santo strolled in wearing his trademark tortoise-frame Wayfarer sunglasses and Dr. Slick gimme ballcap. Ron was a dead ringer for present-day Eric Clapton. Carpenter, handyman, fishing guide, hunter, and font of all things weird and esoteric around here, the sixty year old Santo could do it all. As he often said "I'm a five tool player." We all knew he could play the deepest left field of anyone around and that was saying a lot. Under six feet, lean and fit (The Count and I seemed to be the only slackers in the physical fitness scheme of things), grey hair, glasses, maybe 60 years down the road, always dressed in jeans, a plaid shirt and converse high cut tennis shoes or work boots no matter the occasion or the weather. He also owned a Cessna 182 and claimed he knew how to fly it. This was indeed plausible. He'd been a pilot in the Air Force years ago. And on the arcane side of life he had advanced degrees in electrical engineering from Imperial College London. When asked why that school way over there he said he'd always been interested in the field, the school was one of the best in the world and located not all that far from hallowed chalk streams like the rivers Test, Itchen, Driffield West Beck and Wylye. This made as much sense to the rest of us as anything we'd done while stumbling down the road. He was one of the best anglers on the planet and superb wing shot, personal guide to a couple of famous writers, and superb cook. He was an accomplished individual to say the least. His luck with women was up to par with the rest of us, which is to say decent behavior but dismal success with any relationship lasting more than a couple of weeks. He was an honest, somewhat intense, loyal guy. He was a dear friend to all of us.

"Mind if I grab one of those beers? Asked Santo as he opened the fridge door, pulled out a can and popped the lid, spray and foam shooting all over his shirt and face.

"That must have been the can that dropped off the desk this morning when I was loading the day's supply. Sorry, about that. Have a cigar."

I tend to use a fair amount of wise ass even sarcastic comments to mask my hurt and disgust with many things that happen in my life. It's often easier, a slightly smoother ride interpersonally, to handle my frustrations this way. I don't always have the patience to deal with things like a fully evolved adult and am not all that concerned about the matter. I know who I am and so do my friends. That's what counts.

Santo drained what was left and cautiously opened another. Satisfied he leaned on the wall next to a sketch of a bull trout by at the time local artist Michael Simon. He now lived in Virginia. We all missed the man, who dressed in period outfits, depending on the age of the rod and reel he used on any given day. Plus fours, Tweed caps, shirt and tie, he was a unique one on the stream. The number of tourist's minds he'd blown on the Paradise Valley spring creeks was in the hundreds. And the guy could fish. Michael was a true artist when it came to taking the wily trout with a fly. He was under constant pressure from all of us to move back to Biederbeck, but his Mom was ill and he was taking care of the lady. We all understood the situation.

This ruckus was too much for The Dog who dropped off the couch with a groan, walked into the bedroom/den/kitchen/dining room and curled up on a rug in front of the old fireplace, now obviously dormant. I'd had this restored when I bought the group of rooms that used to be a leather shop/apartment in what is known as the Combination Block Building closing in a century of providing civilized digs for well-heeled derelicts with style and panache. Best money I ever spent. The two of us loved a good fire on a wintry night. The animal was soon snoring. Whenever threatening weather appeared The Dog would abandon the couch or his current spot for the perceived shelter of my claw-foot bathtub, a sturdy piece that came with the place. Thunderstorms, hail, really high wind, fireworks, random gunfire - the tub was his safe house.

Santo came by to kill some time and maybe catch up on any news about not only the murder but current fishing conditions. After angling news – the fishing was poor to nonexistent due to heat and low water, which didn't stop the sports from paying good money to float for miles under a searing sun while going fishless, we filled him in on the crime lab results, shell casings plus our thoughts and conclusions.

"I tend to think along those lines, also," Santo said while helping himself first to another Special Export, that's what they were for – sharing among friends, and then one of my cigars. He lit up and drank some beer before continuing. "Maybe the weapon used was a custom made job that didn't weigh more than a dozen pounds or so and could run off hundreds of rounds a minute. Who the hell knows? Enough money buys anything these days. Feels like a fucking random act done by some out of state asshole. The guy's probably in northern British Columbia by now."

We all more or less agreed and shot the breeze about this and that until The Dog returned at 4 p.m. stared at Santo sitting on the couch until he moved, hopped up, circled twice, collapsed with another groan then turned to me. I grabbed the remote and flicked on the Cubs' game.

"That dog's got you trained slick as can be," said Qualls.

"No shit," said Santo.

"Quite right," said The Count.

We all agreed to meet at Ray's for cocktail hour, which was now looming in the thirsty closing distance. I refilled The Dog's food and water bowls and went to clean up. Another Biederbeck day more or less casually shot in the ass.

***

Ray's was near full with regulars when I walked in. I exchanged pleasantries and wisecracks as I worked my way down the bar with The Dog in tow. He jumped up on his bench, working the quilt around to his satisfaction and assumed his waiting for calamari position – soft eyes, noble profile featuring his enormous ears now at full alert. You could tell this because they hung a quarter-inch away from his head instead of draping his black-and-white head. John Lester was at the bar in the stool next to mine working his way through a large cheeseburger, fries, and a tall glass of beer. A small glass of whiskey was nearly empty.

"Hello Ed," said Lester as he chewed some bun and choice quality beef.

"What an uncommon and pleasant surprise," I said. We

45

shook hands. "Finish eating and I'll work on my drink" He nodded and attacked his burger.

My high ball glass of whiskey was already waiting as I settled in. I caught the bartender's eye and pointed at Lester's drink. Dirt was out of town for the day and night holding court over a showing of some of his latest paintings for the very rich art crowd at the University in Bozeman. He was quite the raconteur and always returned with cash and checks in amounts I'd be afraid to walk around town in the dark with. Not Dirt. He'd stash the money in the bar's safe and slip into his Ray's routine of affability, jocularity and attentive service like he'd never been gone in the first place. The Dog worked away at his squid with a certain delicacy that I felt was more affectation than restraint in a public place. I had started thinking about getting a kitten to keep him on his toes, but the mayhem until the two accepted each other was unthinkable. I'd been down that road in the past and the last time it took two years for dog and cat to settle down – midnight chases and snarling disagreements, overturned vases and other glassware and continual random chaos. I wasn't ready for that right now, if ever again.

A train burdened with a 100 cars or more of coal strip mined from the earth near the Wyoming border at Decker lumbered through town, the six Dash 9 diesel engines pouring smoke as they powered up to take on the grade that climbed the Bozeman Pass. Going up was the easy part, maintaining control of all that tonnage heading down was tricky. Only the most skilled engineers worked this stretch of track. Losing control meant a pileup that would take days to clear, debris closing the I90 and maybe death for engineer and motorist alike, nerve wracking work and not for the faint of heart. The evening breeze was working itself into an uproar if the shuddering plastic pennants on the used vehicles on the lot across the street meant anything.

"She's going to blow tonight and then some," said Lester as he pushed his empty plate away and sipped his drink. I noticed that The Dog already had finished his food and that an order for me was placed off to one side. I nibbled away on calamari after squeezing lemon juice over them and dipping each one in aioli sauce. Like The Dog, I could live on these things.

The bartender, a new guy named David Ross, painting, fly fishing and free climbing were his interests, said "Dirt told me to tell you that your tab is zeroed out and that your money is no good for the time being, Mr. Bouchee."

"Call me Ed, David," I said.

"Nice gig you got going here, Ed" he said without rancor or sarcasm. An athletic, tan, good-looking fellow and about as career orientated as the rest of us. "I think I'm falling in love with this place," Ross added and began working his way back down the line filling drink, cigar and food orders that he relayed to a nearby waitress called Waukonda, lately of the Nightowl. A few weeks ago Dirt offered her more money and better hours. Now she's here. Tough, in her forties, good looking and a straight shooter. We all liked the often testy, but warm-hearted woman. She didn't take any grief from anyone. Dirt said that Waukonda was his de facto bouncer. She and I had been an off and on deal for years and ironically, to my way of looking at the relationship or lack thereof, nothing ever came of our brief times together. I liked Waukonda, liked her a lot. She enjoyed the outdoors especially when we took my 18-foot cedar strip canoe for a spin from town for maybe ten miles downriver to the Otter Access. And she liked to camp, fish, listen to my tastes in music – Radiohead, Coltrane, Danny O'Keefe, Elvin Bishop, Mark-Almond and so on. And she loved my cooking especially my Caesar Salad, Key Lime Cheesecake and Lasagna Bolognese. She and The Dog got along like long lost relations. For some reason, we never managed to stay connected for more than a few weeks at a time. When we parted I immediately missed her kindness, sympathy, laughter and her long, wavy red hair. I guess some things are not meant to be. This one hurt to the point of making me angry at life's unfairness. But then, who ever said life was fair? No one I knew.

The vent fans effectively removed the smoke with a soft drone that was soothing white noise in its own way. Jimmie Dale Gilmore's music was playing through unobtrusive top-end speakers located in near invisible locations. The songs from his *Braver, Newer World* album always got to me in a weird, lonesome way, sort of like traveling through familiar country for the first time. I settled in for a sedate evening and hopefully a long conversation with Lester.

"Anything new on the murders," Lester asked?

I took some time filling him in on Qualls information from this afternoon, The Count's assessment of the shell casings and all of our suppositions. The rancher nodded now and then.

"In other words the cops have got a whole lot of nothing," I said and reached for my drink that had been refilled as if by magic. I was starting to like Dirt's new bartender. Lester's drink was also freshened up. I told Ross to put Lester's food and drinks on my tab.

Ross laughed and said "Remember, your money's no good here right now and that includes reasonable expenses for those you're drinking and talking about the murders with." As he worked down the bar again, I heard him saying in a low voice "Damn, what does this guy have on Dirt," while shaking his head.

Lester and I looked at each and laughed.

"So there are no leads to speak of," said Lester "No suspects and no motives. Really does sound like random murder by someone who's violently insane. Could be a lot of people, even a few I can think of living around here."

"Qualls, the state boys and the FBI have already questioned anyone with even a remotely perceived connection to this," I said. "They all passed muster. As you said, 'No suspects have come to light or moved front and center. Despite the gruesome nature of the murders and the wealth of the victims, I see this one fading into a cold case sunset."

"Maybe an alien spacecraft swooped down from the sky and sprayed those guys with vintage ammunition," I said. "Makes as much sense as anything. I can see Scully and Mulder handling this one on the X-Files."

"Perhaps it does and perhaps there will be a show on this someday," and then Lester started talking about ranching and his family. My questions seemed to lead him from his cattle operation to the story of his brother's death. Or maybe he'd led me to questions that allowed me to think he'd been guided to this area of his life. Screw it. Whatever, Lester's story turned out to be a whole lot more interesting and curious than I would have imagined. This was not just some work-related accident leading to death or even a suicide. This was much more.

"Jim and I weren't what you call real close," Lester began. "We cared for each other, hunted, fished, worked and drank together through the years, but we had our own lives, lives that diverged when we were teens for no apparent reason other than we were born different despite the genes. We had our own way of looking at things and moving through life.

"After Mom died I could tell that Dad wanted both Jim and me to work the ranch with him. He needed help and he was lonely as could be. That was fine with me. I've always loved the place and couldn't imagine doing anything else. Never have. Jim had other ideas. From the first time he went to Yellowstone Park as a kid he was in love with that crazy place – the geysers, mud pots, all the wildlife, natural beauty and even taking in all of the loony tourists and the silly things they did each season. You know, like walking up to an elk or grizzly to take a picture, throwing food in the geysers to watch them cook, feeding the bison, becoming so terrified of driving Dunraven Pass that they stopped their motorhomes in the middle of the road and wouldn't move an inch or look at the edge of the drop off." Lester sipped his whiskey and puffed on a cigar. I did the same and waited for him to continue. "I can't remember how many rigs he told me he had to drive down off that road. The drivers hunkered down in the passenger seat, never looking out the side window at the valley 1,000 feet below. That stretch of road is near 9,000 feet and when wet or icy it's damn dangerous. The Park Service could at least stick a guardrail along the worst of it, if for no other reason than the illusion of safety. Cheap bastards, Jim understood fear, whether it was his own or that in others. That road makes my toes tingle at times, too.

"During the summer months there are all kinds of really stupid things going on that often results in injury or death, Jim liked working through all of it and the challenge of calming a situation down. From the time he graduated high school until his death in 1986 he worked maintenance, mainly roads and trails. Twenty years of it. I'm sixty-two. He would have been sixty this September. He loved every minute, especially the fact that he not only got to see one of the most spectacular places on earth every day, he got paid to do it with full medical including dental and a modest investment program. The fishing can be pretty good up there you know."

"So I've heard, John," I said. "So I've heard." Fly fishing in Yellowstone is known around the world, attracting a who's who of the sport's practitioners including presidents, sports figures and derelict writers of fleeting notoriety and some dignity. I've cast a fly over the place's waters many times and planned to do so countless more days. These are trout waters at their very best.

"I had to agree that Jim made a good choice signing on with the Park Service, but I'd hung my hat on our ranch and I was equally satisfied. Dad was pleased that we were both happy with our career choices and I was happy."

Cocktail hour was more or less over. The bar crowd was down to the regulars, the pros who had a hell of a lot more of nothing to say, usually the same silly BS each night, and plenty of time to do so over drinks. Mostly a quiet, well-healed bunch who moved through the days and nights with a rhythm as predictable as the sun rising and setting each day. Qualls, The Count and Santo had joined us for about 30 minutes at the start of the evening's festivities, then each wandered off to do their own stuff. Qualls was always on call. The Count read and researched whatever came into his head into the early morning hours each night and Santo was always working on some sort of remodeling project either at his place up the Paradise along the river or for some rich out-of-stater's McMansion around here. When he wasn't doing that he was working with his dogs. Best trained and behaved canines on the planet and boy, could they kick up the birds.

We worked steadily on our drinks but not with a 'Let's get hammered' intensity, more a laid back buzz among friends style. As I grow older that's how I like my life. Intensity, craziness and bad trouble find a person easy enough. No point in looking for mayhem. Being dead drunk made things that much more confusing.

"Everything seemed to be going Jim's way. He had a job he loved, government housing at the Mammoth headquarters and meals in the Park when he didn't cook for himself, all of it. He even talked about finding a permanent lady friend, something I've never been able to do in all these years. A month or two of my hard headedness and they seemed to vanish, like smoke on a windy day," said Lester.

"I'm familiar with the situation," I said.

We looked at each other and laughed. There's no helping some of us when it comes to women. That's just the way it is. We're clueless, hopeless, beyond redemption, lacking the patience to make a long-term relationship work.

"Then about two years before he died I noticed a change. It was in the fall of 1984. Jim seemed edgy, angry and a little frightened. He mentioned that a bad element was running loose around the dark edges, his phrase, of Gardiner. That these people were from the coast and they were moving heroin from Canada into this country using the landing strip south of town. What got me is when he said a couple of park rangers were involved including one who flew helicopters on official errands, search and rescues and general observation of the game and backcountry hikers.

Jim added that he was paying attention but keeping things very low key. He heard that a couple of users who had been reported missing over the years were actually murdered because they said too much when they were high or drunk or both at places like The Black Duck in Gardiner. The place is a magnet for low-life's to begin with. The few times I've been in there I felt uncomfortable, like something bad was always on the verge of happening. The place maintains a good front, designer beers, burgers with fancy names, a sound system instead of a juke box, but the druggies use it as a place to make connections. I saw them every time I was in there with their furtive and hard ass looks, the low, sneaky talk. I heard that the ones who talk too much often have their bodies dumped over cliffs above the Yellowstone River in the Mammoth Hot Springs area or buried in the tailings of old mine workings around Jardine up the hill from town. With wild animal foraging, decomposition and spring floods, no trace of their bodies is ever found.

"I told him to stay the hell away from all of the drug bullshit. Life is cheap in that game," Lester said. "Jim assured me that he had things under control, that he was moving well under the drug dealer radar, but he really sounded nervous, even frightened as all get out to me, not himself at all. He didn't laugh anymore, well maybe sarcastically like his life was turning into a bad joke. I think he was in deeper than he was telling me. I couldn't believe that he was a part of any of this or using, but he seemed close enough, too close for me. I tried to get him to take some time off and come up to the ranch, but he said no, that he was busy with the summer tourists. I let it drop. I should have driven down there and helped him out in some way"

"You did your best," I said. "Jim was a big boy and he would have kept you away from the bad things. You wouldn't have seen a damn thing unless he wanted you to."

Hard drug dealing in and around the Park is common knowledge these days. Gardiner, the northern entrance to Yellowstone, attracted every sort of riffraff, especially drug dealers. With over four million visitors to the Park each year it was easy to blend in and get lost in the crowd. Twenty-four years ago much the same must been true. Low life junkies and dealers could easily pass themselves off as youthful outdoor enthusiasts making due from day to day, that is if they so desired. You could be way out and not attract much attention, also. Everyone acts a little bit crazy in national parks, like they're in some giant natural world amusement park. Even with half the number of tourists back in the nineties, they would be just commonplace, itinerant faces in the crowd.

I always figured Gardiner for a drug way station or clearing house, but I never thought park employees would have their hands in the action. Underneath all of the high season visitor lunacy there was a palpable undercurrent of darkness. I avoided the place when I went fishing in the

Park, driving through town and out to the entrance. I went to Yellowstone to fish, not to mingle with a panoply of drugged out losers. But then, rangers or other employees had the perfect cover to do this. Serious money at low risk can tempt any one. Their cover as government employees and access to vehicles, not to mention inside info on law enforcement operations, made the moving of heroin a cinch. Fly Afghan brown in over the border from Canada, say from some out of the way place like Pincher Creek after the junk had been moved in from Vancouver via the Middle East and the dealers were home free. They could distribute the drugs to Casper, Gillette, Denver, anywhere with ease and little chance of detection. Their product was probably far superior, in an addict's eyes anyway, to Mexican tar heroin where users who intravenously inject black tar are at higher risk of venous sclerosis (a condition where the veins narrow and harden, making injection there nearly impossible). Park employees involved in all this made sense to me. This kind of thing was something I'd always avoided. Crossing these people often meant beatings, torture and death. A lame attitude on my part, but I felt that this was someone else's problem. Let the cops handle the drugs. What could I do except get my ass blown away. No thanks.

Lester and I sipped our drinks. Norton Buffalo's Desert Horizon album was now playing, Wonderful, quirky harmonica melodies. Great music. I'd seen him play a number of times, the last ones eight years ago in Whitefish and Bigfork in the northwest corner of the state. Too bad the guy had to die so young from cancer, only 58 years and change. These days 58 was sounding young to me.

"One call from Jim sometime in July of '86 worried the hell out of me. He sounded out of it, like the stress was getting to him and maybe he was drinking a lot," said Lester.

Or maybe he was high on junk himself, spiking the shit

but keeping the habit hidden, I thought. I've known junkies, some of my past friends used or still use the stuff. Many times when not on the nod, they appear relatively normal and more functional than a blackout drunk. The world's become so crazy, so difficult, that being completely fucked up on one's drug of choice does not create the same societal outrage and revulsion that it did in say the "Leave It To Beaver" days or even when the Woodstock generation first overwhelmed the media. I have no idea what half the drugs out there are, let alone what they can do. Times have changed. An old acid freak gone the way of not really hip at all. But then if you think you're hip, you're not. My mind was wandering. I pulled my focus back to the conversation with my rancher friend. Every time I looked at his tan, weathered face the phrase 'salt of the earth' crossed my mind.

"He seemed to think that a local dealer, July Book, was watching him. He described Book as a tall, slim man in his forties with a long greying beard and even longer hair of the same color. Everyone in town stayed clear of the guy. If there was an illegal buck to made in Gardiner, Jardine and the Park, Book was on it in a heartbeat. Bad news all the way around. Book reminded me of a bad character from a Robert Crais novel. He'd been busted for beating the crap out of some tourist kid who mouthed off to him a few years back and did six months in Deer Lodge. Anyone who can survive in that place has got to be tough.

Deer Lodge was a joint where men went to hone their crime skills or to die. A riot there in 1959 ended in three gruesome deaths and a bunch of injuries. It was bad then and the modern replacement prison was worse. A day in there would be an eternal hell for some of us. Guys like Book were a plague, human detritus. These scumbag parasites fed off anyone they could sink their rotten teeth into. Book and his kind would do all of us a favor if they vanished for good. Everywhere they went trouble made an appearance, the bad kind where people were killed or worse.

"Each time Jim went into town, had dinner or drinks at The Black Duck, Antler Pub, Raven Grill or stopped at the Mini Mart, July was there either sitting at the bar or at a corner table or standing off to the side of the places Jim went to. He figured that Book was one of the ones bringing the heroin up from the landing strip outside of town late at night and passing it off to the park service pilot or a ranger who would drive the junk down to Jackson Hole in a YNP pickup, whatever the deal for a specific load was. Jim mentioned that he had put in for a transfer over to Glacier National Park but that this could take months. Paperwork moved slowly in the Park Service, but he'd always been patient. That's a quality we both inherited from Dad.

"I told him to consider taking a leave of absence or possibly quitting until the new position opened up," said Lester "No way he told me. Without the job there was no chance of hitching on at Glacier. Lots of Park Service employees wanted to work there because of the rugged scenery, the nightlife in Whitefish, Columbia Falls and the rest of the Flathead Valley and the quality of life. Even being posted on the East side at St. Mary's or Many Glacier was considered a good deal. Glacier was busy, but not like Yellowstone with only half the number of visitors and far fewer roads. The majority of visitors experienced the Going to the Sun Road through their windshields and that was that."

Whitefish and quality of life in the same sentence. That's a good one.

While the frantic area wasn't Detroit or Mogadishu, the Flathead Valley and Whitefish in particular had gone belly up, sold out to developers, yuppie spawn adventurists, posturing wannabe Buddhists, skiers and the low life flotsam that fed on these people's waste. Gated communities, pretentious art galleries without taste, wildly over-priced restaurants also without taste, golf courses and any type of big-money phony crap a person could imagine, including a large ski resort whose runs had denuded thousands of acres of forest in the Whitefish Range. Traffic gridlock through downtown during the summer months was a common problem. The place was long gone to hell. In many ways Whitefish resembled a poor man's Aspen or Steamboat Springs. Long ago the Flathead Valley was special, wilderness, pristine streams, few people, even in the eighties when I went up there from Missoula to hang out in the woods and mountains up along the North Fork of the Flathead River. Grizzlies, elk, wolves, eagles, bull trout, westslope cutthroat trout, the place had everything for a loner such as myself. I hadn't been over there since I'd seen Norton play at The Remington all those years ago, The Remington was a decent bar-restaurant operation. I doubted if I'd ever be back. Seemed to me that Jim was about to be on the run from a place with its own bad times including hard drugs to another venue with its own set of miseries. Planning this move away from Yellowstone portended of more than casual involvement in the drug trade. The action spoke of fear and desperation.

I ordered another round and prodded Lester to continue.

"What happened next," I asked. "Did you see him before he died or did he at least call again?"

"One last call during the Labor Day weekend. He was excited about the summer tourist rush coming to a close. The Park is still busy in the fall and even the winter, but nothing like summer. The Madison Junction campground is a small city with the same problems – drunkenness, domestic abuse, robbery, health emergencies, even murder. After the first couple of months 'the thrill is gone,' he'd say. Dealing with all the visitors doing the same stupid things over and over wore thin as autumn neared. All the Park employees looked forward to quieter times."

"How did he seem?"

"A lot better," said Lester. "Jim never mentioned the drug problem, Book or anything else negative. He said his transfer had gone through and he'd be moving to West Glacier in early November and would stay in Glacier Park housing at Apgar on Lake McDonald. I've been there. It's a spectacular place. He didn't have a lot of stuff to move – stereo, books, clothes, fishing gear, guns – not much else. All of this would fit in his truck. He seemed in good spirits and laughed when I told him that one of the Prinzgauers got stuck in the muck on the edge of one of our ponds. I had to use the Bobcat and chain to pull the poor thing free. That same damn animal is always getting stuck in something, fences, mud, wedged in a gate, you name it. Those cows have more ways of wasting my time than government Ag agents with all their foolish regulations that they're always amending. A fella can't keep up with all the government nonsense. Jim suggested that I butcher the entire heard and sell the meat to the outfit in Butte we always did business with."

"I can see why I realized a long time ago that ranching wasn't for me," I said. "Too much work all day every day."

Lester looked at me before saying, "You might be better at it than you think. If you ever need work and a place to stay, you've got one."

I was touched, truly touched by this offer and must have looked a touch choked up.

"Don't go all bullshit new age, touchy feely on me," Lester said. "You're a bit long in the tooth, but I'd find a way to get a full day's work out of you. Room, board, a little money and all the fishing you can handle would be the pay."

We let this offer of ranch work drift off with our cigar smoke, but I'd keep it in mind. We turned back to Jim's story.

"I never saw or heard from my brother again," said Lester. "On the morning of September 21ˢᵗ, right after the full moon, something I always keep track of for no particular reason, I got a call from an official at the Park Service asking me if I'd seen Jim. I said no and asked why. I was told that he'd failed to show up for work for two days and nobody had seen him since he left work before the weekend. They all thought he'd driven up to the ranch to do some bird hunting with me."

"A full search got underway with the county boys looking in O'Keefe County and the Biederbeck police running checks everywhere in town. After a week when nothing had turned up – no live Jim, no dead Jim, no clues and no leads, all of the agencies scaled back their efforts. During that time I drove thousands of miles checking out places no one but Jim and I knew about and plenty of obvious ones like put ins on the river, places we'd camped and spots we hunted in the past. I even checked with the outfit we sold beef to in Butte on the chance he went there for some crazy reason. Nothing. Qualls and various Park officials interviewed me several times.

"After a month the case went cold, almost dead," said Lester as he finished another drink that was immediately refilled. "I worked the bars in Gardiner including The Black Duck. Nothing up there either and I got the impression that the town was sick and tired of the questions and the presence of the cops. One night at The Black Duck I overheard some kids, maybe in their early twenties, talking about Book and how he probably did in Jim because he was asking questions about moving heroin in the area."

"Then what?" I asked finishing my drink which was immediately refilled? I could get used to this treatment by Ross.

"I went back to their table, introduced myself and tried

to find out anything I could. All of them knew and liked Jim and said how sorry they were about his death. He hadn't been officially declared dead, but with no body or anything else in nearly a month, they were only saying what the cops and I thought. Apparently Book left town right after Jim's disappearance in his pickup that was loaded with all his gear, such as that was. A Ranger in the Mammoth area had quit suddenly and moved back east. Makes me wonder, but I never turned over anything else. I told O'Keefe County sheriff, a guy named Ken Keltner. The guy died of a massive heart attack when one of his deputies walked in on him screwing the office secretary on his desk. Strange way to check out.

"I remember the incident. That's when Qualls was elected to replace Keltner in a special election in 2007," I said.

"Yes, that's how that happened. At the time Keltner checked into all of this, even running Book's truck plate. Nothing. No sign of the guy anywhere. The retired park ranger was in a hospital being treated for pancreatic cancer. He died two months after Jim vanished, so I guess that was a dead end. Keltner did a thorough job, was real understanding and helpful. Whatever people think about the way he died, I found him to be a good man."

"I did too. We were friends of a sort. Even went fishing and bird hunting with him a few times. I made sure I never got in the way of his job and he told me he respected that," I said.

"So that's the condensed version of Jim's disappearance or death, but you can fill in the blanks and most likely when you do, you'll be where I am right now."

"Like I said awhile back about something else, I forget what, I've been there with these situations," I said.

We worked on our drinks. Radiohead's King of Limbs was now playing. Great way out there music that Waukonda liked and called "mondo." Okay, mondo it is then. I wasn't familiar with the details of Jim's death. I'd talk with Dirt about all this. What he didn't know about the town's history. He could find out. If I wanted more, Santo was next on my list. For now I'd let all of Lester's story rattle around in my head and possibly sort itself out some.

"'So since then for almost 22 years nothing on Jim. He's gone, vanished like he never existed," I asked.

"That's about the size of it. Makes me mad as hell to think about all of this or talk about his death with you," said Lester. "I didn't realize that I'd miss him so much. And my patience about some things is shot to hell and back like those three murdered men. They had it coming, the bastards. Buying up land and closing it off to all of us for the sake of a buck. The neighboring ranch I mentioned is a good example. They backed up a spring creek that also ran through my land. Used to hold brown trout that made it all the way up from the Yellowstone long before people settled this country. Now they're gone. Made an earthen dam to back up the water and form a trout pond, then filled the thing with hatchery rainbows for the rich assholes that fish and hunt there. I had to go to court to sue for them to honor my water rights on the stream. We'd held them since the family bought the place. We won but what water doesn't evaporate or seep back in the ground is nothing more than a swampy trickle on my land. And they have orange no trespassing sprayed on every wooden post on their land. Fine neighbors they are. Makes me want to beat all hell out of people like that, but then I'm too damn busy chasing cows to take the time."

He sounded more than angry, outraged better described his attitude, but when I looked up from my drink his eyes were sparkling and that lightning crease of a smile made me smile. We chatted for a little while longer about the day to day before Lester said he had to leave. The drive back to the ranch was more than an hour. We'd had a fair amount to drink but Lester looked sober as a judge even if he wasn't. Biederbeck. I walked with Lester back to his Power Wagon, shook hands, said that I'd see him again real soon. He drove off and I tottered back to my place. Two paved blocks, but not as easy as it looked. I watered, fed and showered attention on The Dog. Then we both went to sleep.

***

Late summer, late night. Full moon. The prairie sailed away forever in all directions beneath silver light bright enough to throw thick black shadows. The eroded bluffs, sage brush, cattle and the distant mountains cast elongated shadowy silhouettes of themselves upon the land. Nighthawks boomed and rushed through the night riding the warm breeze. Antelope and elk grazed peacefully within the serene August night. The ungulates steady munching a mild counterpoint to the birds hunting insects. Cattle stand motionless, still life images scattered about the tranquil scene. A pair of glowing white orbs dance, jump and rotate around two eroded cones in the east, shapes formed long ago when the area was still influenced by magma flowing beneath the earth's surface. The balls of lightning are an uncommon form of St. Elmo's Fire. A low sizzling sound emanates from each run, the noise vanishing as each diaphanous object spins out of sight, returning again and again as a supernatural mixture of light, sound and motion. Their appearance heralds an approaching storm sometime later tomorrow. For now all is peaceful.

A restored Fokker D.VII was illuminated in the yellow-orange light of several kerosene lanterns hanging from roof beams in the hanger. The biplane's owner was putting the last preparations for tomorrow's flight to bed – topping off fuel, arming the twin Maxim machine guns with 500 round belts of Privi Partizan 7.65x53mm ammunition, checking

62

engine oil levels, cleaning the wind screen, the taut fabric wing surfaces, the fixed two-wheel landing gear and checking all of the rigging one more time. He also spent time admiring the lines of the aircraft and its maize and blue colorings marked distinctively with the long, white dragon herald. He'd finished the restoration a year ago after thousands of hours of research and work.

The facelift of all the plane's surfaces, the tooling of replacement parts including those for the engine took patience and skill in order to reproduce them identical to the originals of nearly a century before when German fighter pilot Wilhelm Leusch flew the original of the plane in the hanger for Royal Prussian Jagdstaffel 19, a hunting squadron stationed not far from the front. The man who had invested so much time in the restoration and reconstruction of the Fokker – original frame, engine and parts bought from a farmer in Bavaria whose father had salvaged the downed aircraft after The Great War, the one that was purported to end all such madness. The cost was not inexpensive when the shipping to its hanger in central Montana was factored in. The new owner, this man standing alone in the hidden hanger, often felt like he was the German pilot at times. Working on the D.VII changed the man's makeup, fused him with the plane and its noble but deadly past. This shift into a different identity from a pilot long dead was abrupt, clearly noticeable in the beginning. As time passed the transition was seamless as though both personalities were different sides of the same person. It took the light of a new day's sunrise to bring him back to the man the contemporary world thought he was. His friends thought of him as a regular guy, "an ordinary Joe," is how he put it in his head when he considered such things, less common as time moved on. He knew he was now also a killer. Not a murderer, a righteous man of vengeance that brooked no moderating or tempering dialogue from his fading conscience. There was more work to do, more killing. He had no idea how many would die. He operated on information that fueled impulses unmeasured but oddly calculated.

It took him years to find a serviceable pair of LMG 08/15 machine guns. He'd spent weeks machining damaged or worn parts and more hours firing them and fine tuning them until they were as good as when they'd been finished at the government arsenal in Spandau, Germany. He carefully hooked the guns and synchronizer to the plane's BMW IIIa engine so, when fired, the bullets would pass between the spinning propellers and not shoot it off. He replaced the original and quite heavy fuel tank with a larger yet much lighter aluminum one that greatly increased the D.VII's range. He'd modified the landing gear and ordered special tires to accommodate the rough rock of his landing strip. Many more tasks were completed one by one until the intensive restoration project was completed and he took his machine for its initial flight on a night similar to this one in mid-May of last year. After many more outings of a couple of hours each, done always under the cover of darkness, he was no longer merely the plane's pilot. He was part of this acrobatic, powerful killing machine. He was ready to put his plane and his planned retributions into action. The first stage, shooting the men who had destroyed so much of Montana, was complete, He'd shredded their bodies while they floated the Yellowstone River two weeks ago on a blue sky, hot July afternoon. Tomorrow he would complete his second mission at a location in the mountains rising in the west, the ones he could see in the moonlight at this moment, the jagged peaks looking like the shining teeth of an ancient predator.

He removed latex gloves, extinguished the lanterns, slid the hanger doors shut and locked them. He paused to take in the evening, the velvet feel of the air, the stars shining brightly outside the sphere of influence cast wide by the glowing moon. Two meteors, one after the other, sizzled across the sky and exploded not many miles from where he stood, the light of these briefly turned night into day. A pair of muffled booms racing across the open land reached his ears. A pack of coyotes howled from a ridge in the south, either frightened or acknowledging the power of the natural world as so fiercely displayed by the meteors. Their vocals modulated in pitch, starting low then rising higher and higher before ending with abrupt, low-pitch yelps. The man mimicked their calls. There was silence, then the animals answered back. He smiled as he walked towards his home.

Tomorrow would be a good day. He was certain of this.

***

I never tired of watching Dirt work a stream. In his hands a vintage bamboo fly rod was at once a combination of grace, accuracy and power melded into a combination of casting efficiency that was pure art. The rod would flex parabolically when he lifted the fly line from the surface film continuing backwards over Dirt's right shoulder before returning to bend forward as he brought his hand towards the spot on the water he was aiming for, the fly line a tight loop that shot forward at high speed before being abruptly checked to drop with a fine delicacy on the surface. The small fly would land on the water in the perfect spot without spooking the fish, float a few feet before being inhaled by a wild trout, that Dirt would play fairly and quickly before bringing the fish to hand. He would admire the riot of colors, the streamlined muscular body and then release the Yellowstone cutthroat that swam away rapidly and disappeared, blending in with the brightly-colored streambed. Then Dirt would turn his attentions to the next aquamarine pool or bankside run and repeat the process. Photos or videos of the guy on the water could not capture the beauty and poetry of this. I never tried, preferring to store all the fantastic images in my mind, images that aged, cured and developed over time into memories I called up whenever the dark, cold blues of winter or life in general came calling.

Last night at Ray's we made plans to head up this way around 9 a.m. to fish and shoot the breeze about last month's murders. Dirt was eager to hear what I'd learned.

August 19th, late morning, the headwaters section of a stream created from ice and snow melt from the snowfields a couple of thousand feet above us. Tiny springs made their offerings in liquid tricklings wherever water bubbled up from beneath the ground along the way down the foothills. By the time all of this had flowed down through forest, gorge and open field the stream had evolved into a modest river. This was the day after last night's full moon. The weather was insanely good, a mixture of high summer with a touch of the crispness and clarity of the approaching fall season. We liked to fish the day after a full moon, not because the action was any better. We did so because we enjoyed pretending that the trout were more eager, that we understood aspects of fishing others were unaware of, kids playing a game of pretend. Life was fun like this. Each of us was in our early fifties, but decades ago we both waited for the feeling of being a real adult, dominated by character traits of being responsible, dutiful, gruff and miserable (we did possess these dubious qualities but in measured quantities). No thanks. We weren't interested in buying into this emotional death trip con. We often referred to our condition as childlike, carefree and without hope or redemption on the "Maybe they'll grow up someday" front. The train had left the station for good on that one a long time ago. I silently prayed that none of this way of seeing the world would ever change. Maybe the powers that be had cut the two of us a big break. Maybe we were among the lucky ones roaming the planet. I caught myself and ended this line of thought. I didn't want to jinx a fine thing.

Dirt caught and released a few more small trout and then splashed his way back across the high mountain stream to the large grey deadfall I was sitting on. The air smelled of pine and the cool water. A light breeze pushed softly through the tree tops creating a cushioned sigh. Mountain chickadees flitted from limb to limb chirping away. A vulture soared high above us riding the thermals from peak to peak here in the Norton Mountains, our favorite island mountain range in the world, a self-contained amusement park, wonderland and magic show all rolled into one. Dirt and I knew we were blessed and the word grateful didn't come close to explain how we felt. Pale morning dun mayflies the size of small buttons rose off the stream's surface, looping and circling in their mating dance. Their wings flickered in the sunlight – long lives as nymphs underwater, then a short run to the surface and a leap into the air to breed and die all within hours. A metaphor for all our lives.

The Dog, after running and swimming through a swampy side channel, returned a complete mess. One of his endearing qualities is that he would not wait and shake water and detritus on me after romping in the woods and creeks. He unburdened himself of the excess moisture well away from humans. I liked him all the more for this un-canine-like trait. He was lying on his stomach, head resting on outstretched paws snoring loudly.

"I could use a brief lie down myself," said Dirt. "Didn't sleep much at all last night. Too many things running through my head, like the killings on the river."

After Dirt settled in on a smooth, rounded spot on the grey wood next to me, he pulled a pair of cigars from an old leather case he'd picked up in Havana while down there selling his art to a local collector. He also found time to visit the Havana cigar factories and the tobacco plantations around Pinar del Rio in the Vuelta Abajo. He'd found the fishing off the nearby western coast to be poor, saying the people who lived there fished the waters hard due to frequent shortages of meat in the region and had worked the waters near shore, the reefs and sand flats, out for the most part. He handed me a cigar. After clipping and lighting them we took our time enjoying the surroundings. Then as always, as if by magic, Dirt's antique silver flask appeared sparkling in the light of midday. In all the years and all the times I've fished and bird hunted with my friend I never once captured the moment when this object was removed from a shirt or pants pocket. The Scottish museum quality piece that Dirt acquired from an untold source when fishing for brown trout and shooting red grouse in the Scottish Highlands seemed to just be there, appeared as though it were a prop in some esoteric act of legerdemain. Today the capricious item held an Irish whiskey whose taste I knew well. Dirt purchased several cases of the liquor at great expense two Christmases ago from a writer friend who lived in Key West. The writer, an individual of some renown in literary circles, had more than enough to last him for a good while, so Dirt accepted his generous though lofty offer. I took a decent swallow, savoring the flavors of smoky peat, heather, aged wood and alcohol.

"Have another," Dirt said. "I've got two flasks with me, the twin of the one you're holding. I spotted it on a Christie's auction online and paid dearly for it. Cost be damned, I wanted the thing."

I did as I was told and had another taste. Fine stuff that went perfectly with the Montecristo Especial No. 2s we were smoking. Conversation revolved around this stream, the fish and the glorious day before our talk wandered into the land of the murders Dirt, hell all of us, were so curious about.

"What have you learned about the killings in the last

month," he asked? "Fill me in and I'll answer any questions or expand on local knowledge related to all this. Please be so kind as to fill in any interstitial gaps you can."

"Interstitial?"

"I came across the word in a novel by Bob Jones, I think it was *Tie My Bones To Her Back*. Like the sound of the word. Seems to fit in here."

"Okay, Dirt," I said. He could have his word. I'll enjoy his whiskey, seemed a fair exchange.

I told Dirt about the shell casings I'd found in the river down below the murder site, my dust up with the two FBI agents, along with the information on the casings provided by The Count including ballistics and possible gun makes. I filled him in on what Qualls told us during the same meeting, the sheriff relating that there was not a single suspect, no one with motive, means and opportunity and that even the few with one of the three identifiers, usually anger as the potential motive over some slick business scheme, provided stone cold alibis. The victims' computers and cell phones were dead ends also. Checking websites visited by the three and their partner, Twiggy Hartenstein, turned up nothing other than an apparently strong interest in porn sites shall we say of an arcane nature. Calls made from all of the men's various phone numbers were also fruitless, amounting to nothing more than business, day to day matters and female companions None of them were married and little if any close family ties, though the few tenuous familial connections were looked into and discarded as still more dead ends.

"Qualls called this morning and told me the shell casings were a wash as far as discovering any DNA," I said. That the only DNA there was to work with was from the remains, and they'd already been identified through dental. I guess the Ids are now double confirmed. Blind alleys and dead ends are the signatures of these killings.

"Qualls had added that his office was the only law enforcement agency actively involved in the matter at this time, and that's about all I know."

Nothing else.

"Well, Qualls did mention that the FBI and state police had their hands full with the lame ass Freemen wannabes up Jordan way in the far eastern middle of nowhere Montana."

Eight of them had taken over an abandoned wildlife survey station vowing to fight it out to the death if their demands weren't. So far no demands had been made, at least not publicly. This was a bunch of whiny, gun toting clowns who took advantage of every government entitlement program possible and every tax break imaginable, and some not quite believable, at least by those few that held legitimate jobs. On the other hand they pissed and moaned about how the government was making their lives hell, and planned to confiscate all their guns, which were many, and take their land through eminent domain. These inbred imbeciles had been sucking at the federal tit since day one of their lives and bitching about it all the way down the line. I hoped the FBI and state cops cleaned up on this latest collection of riff raff with dispatch and alacrity so they could put some pressure to bear on the slaughter on the Yellowstone, a bad deal that made all of us nervous whenever we went fishing, canoeing or just walking along what we thought of as our river.

"I agree with you on the latest iteration of the Freeman in our state, Ed," said Dirt. "Throw the bunch of them in Deer Lodge Prison for a little dose of real tough times state pen style, and take their land and guns for good measure. Show those fools what due process really means out this way. Or maybe stick them in Warm Springs Mental Hospital and keep them loaded on Prolixin."

"Dirt, you do realize that our world views such as they

may be might tend to upset the politically correct sheep wandering so terribly lost in this great land of ours," I said. "Don't you think the tender souls need our kindness and consideration too?"

Dirt took a hit from the flask and passed what I now considered one of his many fly fishing totems over to me. I took a slash. Definitely top shelf liquor.

"Fuck 'em," he said around a modest belch. "And the horse they rode in on. I guess my dream of being on the watered down travesty they call The Tonight Show or even on Oprah is long gone."

If only the PCers who bought up Dirt's paintings with nary a thought to the price he put on them could hear their sensitive artist now. But they wouldn't and as my crazy bass playing brother-in-law Lemmy would say, "It's all good," but that's a story for another day and definitely not for the faint of heart.

"I can see that you're on one of your puerile digressions into the realm of some obscure strain of hubris," said Dirt.

"No, just thinking a bit."

"Like I said, Ed. Like I said."

Having adequately vented our emotions on these subjects, we settled down and enjoyed the whiskey and cigars while we watched the little cutthroat splashing and chasing the mayflies now with slightly large caddisflies mixed into the whirling insect dance. As we took in the display I described my visit to Lester's ranch a couple of weeks back – the general, good natured conversation along with the fishing and my spending the night there after an evening of R&R fueled talk. I detailed the rancher's love of flying in his crop duster. I retold Lester's tale of how his brother vanished and or died nearly 32 years ago mentioning every detail down to July Book, The Black Duck, the park service and all the stuff about the heroin.

Dirt mulled all this over as he went back to the stream,

71

made two delicate roll casts to a smooth run beneath some arbor vitae trees and took cutthroat with each skillful effort. The fish were several inches longer than those he fooled earlier. Over his shoulder he said, "I spotted those two when I first stepped in earlier, but spooked them so I allowed plenty of time to forget my intrusions. What's the length of a trout's memory cycle? Thirty-one minutes or something."

"If the prey tastes bad or is in itself dangerous up to 24 days for brown trout," I modestly offered.

"Lord God almighty, you're full of shit, Ed," said Dirt. He turned back to fishing muttering "Twenty-four hours. Where does he get this stuff?"

When he returned, he looked at me with an expression that was equal parts wry grin and satisfaction. He sat down on the tree once again and handed me a flask that was identical to the one we'd nearly emptied. I never saw it coming.

"How do you do that?" I asked. "I'm driving myself nuts trying to figure your little gimmick out."

"Ed, you and I were born nuts, the switch was clicked on at birth. It's no gimmick. Like many things that sail over your head in this life, you need to learn how to see without looking."

I chose to ignore this metaphysical jive whenever it appeared between us. I was a lifelong Cubs fan and was well versed in the harsh realities of life. None of Dirt's lofty aphorisms cut it with me. I had enough trouble seeing while looking. Instead I asked, "Any questions or anything to add or fill in on my research?"

"Most of what Lester told you is right on," said Dirt. "He went through a rough patch following the deaths of his mom, dad and brother in what seems to me to be a relatively short time. He hit the sauce hard for several months before pulling that back together. In town he was often angry, curt and morose, but all that went away with the passing of time and his getting the booze under control, at least as controlled as any of us can in this loony tunes world. Did he really say that they'd never recovered Jim's body?"

"Yes and it was obvious that this was eating him up."

"Two park rangers found Jim's body on the kitchen floor of his apartment in Mammoth with a needle in his arm holding a small mixture of blood and drugs," said Dirt. "A blackened spoon used for the cooking was on the floor. Dried saliva on his face. He'd pissed himself and worse. A lovely sight I'm sure. Death had been two days prior from a drug overdose according to the Medical Examiner who's done his share of OD post mortems from up Gardiner way. The examiner said that Jim had needle tracks on both arms and starting up a vein on his right leg. He'd been shooting that junk for some time. No one, including that scumbag Book, murdered him. He killed himself. It seems that Lester has never been able to admit his brother's addiction. Not uncommon. We all lie to ourselves about one thing or another. Human nature. Nothing sick or sinister. It's just how most of us are wired."

"What the hell," I said. "I was stunned. Either Lester was lying to me or was extremely delusional about a few little items in his life."

"Like I just said," added Dirt with a grim laugh. "Don't read too much into it. Telling you this, even the deluded parts, more than likely helped Lester blow off some steam. A tough man like that would be a son-of-a-bitch to deal with if he ever blew his stack. I wouldn't want to be within ten miles of him if that happened."

I looked up the timbered valley into the blue sky crease that opened up to a mountain lake on the other side and thought, 'I wouldn't want to be in Lester's neighborhood at such a time either.'

"I'm more inclined with each passing day to think that this was the work of some homicidal maniac who got the urge, saw the opportunity out here in the wild, wild west and killed the three in the raft," said Dirt. "This could be as simple as that. The killer might turn up through something as routine as a traffic stop and then it's 'Case solved.' Good grief, John Lester makes as good a suspect as any of us around here. And it's not him."

"Maybe it's your new bartender," I said.

"David has trouble tying his shoes and walking a straight line on any level. He does the job behind the bar and never misses a shift, something not all that common in the Biederbeck work force, the use of the term work force is a generous one."

"Do want me to continue with this for a while longer," I asked? "There's something in the back of my mind that's bothering me. If the little detail or details ever surface, I have a feeling that I might be on to something."

"Stay with it," Dirt said. "You and that Dog aren't going to eat and drink me out of business," and my friend punched me of the left shoulder and broke wind. "At least that still works."

I belched. "So does that."

Like I mentioned, little kids at work here.

"One last thing Qualls told me," I said. "The state police stopped a Cadillac Escalade for doing 103 miles per hour near the top of Lookout Pass right at the Idaho line. Two men in the vehicle and when they ran each of them they had warrants for armed robbery, felony assault and a bunch of drug violations. A search turned up to Mac 10s, a Glock 10mm and a sawed off twelve gauge. They were both white males, runners for the Mexican Sinaloa cartel. Chump change in the grand scheme of drug dealing."

"Wrong calibers," said Dirt. "Not the shooters at the river."

"Agreed, but the kicker is they had enough heroin, over fifty kilos, to light up Spokane for months. Like Qualls said, a good bust, but not our guys. No other stops in the state or nearby areas turned up anything other than the usual white trash mayhem – stolen cars, parole violations, unlicensed weapons of the wrong caliber, DUIs. The usual. I'm starting to truly believe that whoever killed the three on the river are long gone and obviously damn good at flying under the radar."

"Al of this going nowhere," said Dirt. "But keep at it. I keep having a feeling that something will break and right around town. Just a hunch, but you know how those usually play out."

I did. My friend had an uncanny knack for flashing on things that no one else saw coming. Like the magical flasks, this was just another of his arcane, mysterious abilities. If Dirt said something on the murders would pop up, I believed him. I'd stay with the investigation for a little while longer.

We stood up with the intention of fishing some pools that ran in a series along a rock cliff a few hundred yards upstream, when sounds of distant gunfire, a lot of it shattered the forest calm. Seconds later an enormous explosive sound echoed down the valley, the shockwaves hurting my eardrums. Then another one, equally concussive reached us. The force of this pushed the limbs of the tallest trees around us like they'd been caught in a sudden gust of wind. Dead and green pine needles sifted down to the forest floor.

We looked at each other and were speechless. What just happened? Did a LP tank truck explode delivering fuel to the lodge that was being renovated on the mountain lake less than a mile away on the other side of the mountain saddle that marked the beginning of this drainage we were fishing? Had someone been careless with rifle fire and touched off a case of explosives like Semtex or dynamite? I'd heard that the new owners, in addition to modernizing the lodge that was built in the 1930s, were blasting out rock outcroppings to shorten and widen the narrow rock, dirt and gravel road into the place. Big game season was fast approaching. Montana hunters lived for this and spent hours sighting in their weapons, so the report from seemingly random gunfire was not uncommon at this time of the year. A bullet gone astray, a shattered ricochet, may have touched off stored explosives.

Several smaller explosions rocked the air. Then we both noticed a biplane circling to gain altitude just on the other side of the dip in the ridge that gave way to the valley, lake and lodge, barely above the tree tops the plane banking sharply up and to the east. The harsh sound of its engine seemed to crackle around us, drowning out the sound of the stream. In the early afternoon light the plane looked to be off-yellow and deep blue with a white vertical rudder marker with a black cross. The sun was to the south and a little west of the craft so the machine's features were illuminated as though by an open-faced light fixture used in film making. Even from this distance, maybe 1,200 feet, I could make out what looked like a white, long-tailed dragon painted on the blue fuselage. The pilot wore goggles and gloves. A long, blue and yellow scarf stretched behind him like a pennant. I could see twin guns mounted just ahead of the cockpit. The vintage plane, vintage because its design looked quite old to my eyes, soon disappeared over the uneven mountainous horizon, as it did so the engine noise faded away too.

"That's a Fokker D, VII, I'll bet my ass on it." Said Dirt who is an expert on many things arcane and esoteric. "And it's painted in Wilhelm Leusch's colors and insignia. Son of a bitch. A long dead German ace flies again."

I had no idea what he was talking about. I didn't care at this point. We needed to hoof it down the trail back to the rig and our cell phones to call this in. I was willing to bet medical aid was dearly needed just over that ridge, and some cops wouldn't hurt either.

I noticed The Dog crouched beneath the dead tree. The poor little guy was shivering with fear. I reached down and rubbed his ears and head and told him, "It's okay now, buddy. Don't worry." He looked up at me. The look said he was buying my line and wanted to get the hell out of here and back home where it was safe, mostly likely curled up in the bathtub. I looked at Dirt with what must have appeared to be shock and horror. He returned the stare, a look of concern and anger covering his face.

"Not again," he said. Not fucking again."

***

About an hour before noon he launched the Fokker D.VII into the clear blue sky following the rough roll out on the gravel and dirt runway that cleared a six-foot wall of sage brush by several dozen feet. The iron tough plants sheltered the air strip from wind-blown tumbleweed when the weather came in from the southwest, the predominant direction during the warmer months of the year. The restored WWI biplane fighter climbed easily and swiftly into the sky reaching an altitude of 8,000 feet quickly. In 1918 the Fokker D.VII was considered the deadliest aircraft of the war, maneuverable, powerful, well-armed. Though by today's standards the D.VII was barely a pee shooter compared to modern fighters, the plane was still capable of dispensing lethal force and enormous destruction when left alone to do its bidding. The pilot counted on stealth and a surprise attack and then a swift exit from the crime scene and a return to the isolated landing strip way out in the middle of Montana nowhere. Flying to and from the attack site using the cover of timbered canyons and then flying barely above the desiccated loneliness of the prairie, he felt confident that he would go unobserved. If seen, he doubted anyone would be able to recognize the type airplane he was in, let alone identify its owner, since he'd only flown in daylight one time previously. All of his dozens of other excursions had been at night. He was confident in his success and maintaining his anonymity.

The vast openness of the plains stretched out beneath the lower wing. The engine roared with unfettered power cruising along at 120 mph. During the climb to altitude the noise of the motor spooked a herd of antelope grazing on the rim of a coulee that ran out from the Norton Mountains. The buck looked up, then scooted down country to the east with his twelve does in tow. They vanished in seconds within the thick brush and shadows cloaking the bottom of the cut in the land. The animals were adept at surviving in the harsh countryside.

Several vultures, six-foot wingspan, red heads and all, rode the thermals to the north gliding higher and higher above the land that was now late summer brown except for a few emerald creases in the isolation where springs and the last traces of glacial cirque snowmelt nourished the ground in small wrinkles in the landscape. Ahead, the peaks of the Nortons loomed like an ancient buttress to a hidden fortress constructed of silver-grey rock that cast purple shadings in the atmospheric haze. The tallest peaks were 10,000 feet and change. He'd clear them with ease before swooping down the western slopes and powering in on his target. The pilot had all of this vastness to himself, no other planes or commercial jets would be making their approaches to Bozeman fifty miles distant. The common glide path for this was more than thirty miles to the south. He'd already crossed over the little-used two lane highway running north and south. There'd been no traffic. There were no roads to fly over, only dusty two-track affairs made over time by pickups and farm equipment that rolled and curved far into remote sectors of the area's ranches. At this altitude the temperature was less than fifty degrees Fahrenheit. He was glad he'd worn his leather coat, calfskin gloves and leather helmet. He was equally glad he'd taken a couple of pulls on the flask of brandy he carried with him before the flight. The castor fumes from the engine lubricants often produced nausea and laxative-like effects. The liquor helped prevent these deleterious conditions.

Despite the cramped cockpit filled with all sorts of levers, pedals and gauges, the pilot felt alive in a way he never did when down on the ground, though he loved the many thousands of acres of land he owned and knew and understood perhaps far better than he did himself. There was a freedom, a detachment from the world of these frantic times. No road rage, cell phones, televisions spewing the nonstop blather of network news automatons. The feeling of freedom often became visceral, much like cresting an abrupt hill on a highway going over one-hundred-miles-an-hour.

As he climbed up through an ice-scoured canyon towards the peaks above he looked down at a trio of alpine lakes resting like gems in a swampy meadow, forested on the foothill side and barren where they butted up to the rugged cliffs and scree slopes. A sow grizzly and two cubs frolicked along the outlet creek of the highest lake The silvery adult displayed a well-defined hump along its shoulders. The fur rippled and glistened in the intense sunlight. The powerful animals looked up at the Fokker as the wicked craft powered by only a few hundred feet above as the pilot maneuvered to clear an approaching knife-like ridge and descend towards his target, less than ten miles distant. The bears followed his trajectory with their large heads until the Fokker zipped over the ridge before slipping down below the rock wall. The bears went back to the serious business of playing and feeding on mountain huckleberries. Time was short. Winter at this altitude often comes in October. The need to gain body mass, a thick layer of fat to tide them through the bitter cold months of hibernation was intense, an instinctual imperative that dominated the moves of the mother. She would allow only so much play among her cubs before sternly scolding and driving them into the bushes now full of ripe purple berries.

The U.S. Fish and Wildlife Service and the Forest Service adamantly claimed to anyone who was within shouting range that the Nortons were an island mountain range, and that the only bears in the mountains were black bears and not grizzlies. Most area ranchers knew otherwise from empirical experience gleaned over decades – ravaged beehives, mangled calves, destroyed fence lines, not to mention personal sightings and confrontations. Men of the high plains were well aware of the differences between black bears and grizzlies. The reason for the obvious distortion or outright abrogation of this natural truth by government officials was simple. To admit that a viable population of the great bears made these mountains their home would force the Forest Service to stop all logging in the area, along with exploration for possible mineral and natural gas deposits, not to mention oil and coal. Preserving this environment for the endangered bears was federal law. Grizzlies are a protected species. The pilot was aware of this and he was also aware of the painful fact that economics trumped biology and preserving the animals in this location. He didn't mind losing a few of his cows, or some honey or fixing a fence line if it meant he could share his land with grizzlies, to actually have at least the illusion of interaction with the species.

"Assholes," he said through a blue and maize scarf wrapped around his mouth and neck. "Complete assholes."

Grizzlies sometimes wandered far out onto the prairie or was it plains. Such minor distinctions annoyed the hell out of the pilot. Prairie or plains. Plains or prairie. Good country is good country. Simple as that. Case closed.

Whenever he considered such malfeasance by government agencies, the pilot went a little bit crazy, often thinking violent thoughts about not only the USFS and USFWS but also the Park Service. Somebody should shoot the bastards he'd think.

He shook his head vigorously to clear it of these distracting thoughts and refocused on the task that was fast approaching, The blue-green lake grew in size. Even his target, an old lodge built twenty years before he was born, was now visible as a brown series of one large rectangle and several smaller connected shapes. Yellow-silver light reflected off small waves on the water and off the building's windows.

The pilot skillfully and abruptly dropped the fighter down to tree top level, prop wash buffeting tree tops shaking loose aspen leaves and cones from the tops of tall pines. He could see the lodge in some detail now – the two men working on installing a new shake roof, their work truck parked around back near a large white propane tank that supplied the gas for all the places' needs, a new dock thrusting forty feet into the lake with an eleven-foot Boston Whaler powered by a 15 horsepower Mercury and a cedar strip canoe. Nice boats the pilot thought in passing. The front of the lodge gave way through a series of tall sliding glass doors to a large cedar deck outfitted with high end chairs, tables and lounges. As he closed in he spied a massive field stone cooking station with a seven-point elk rack mounted on top. Bundles of shakes were stacked between two ladders. He could see a smooth, wide, well-graded road leading from a circle in front of all of this around the west shore of the lake and disappearing in a wide bend around some large hills before breaking free of the dense old growth timber far below where it ran across open fields and along a creek. The pilot knew who owned this place or used to own it and all about the obscene prices they charged their wealthy clientele to stay here, up to a $1,000 a day. Three of the four owners were dead. He'd shot them all to hell and back on the Yellowstone River almost a month to the day during his first ride to vengeance. He had the fourth on his list of things to see and do. The fulfillment of his second operation was at hand. He adjusted the Fokker's flight path into a gradual downward angle to bring the twin Maxim machine guns to bear on the lodge, the truck and finally the propane tank. Using a tool of his own making based on a century-old Kingston Device, he cocked the guns with one hand while maintaining flight trim with his other hand on the stick and his booted feet on the pedals. The D.VII screamed in on its targets now less than 1,000 yards away.

He pulled the trigger control in the cockpit and the Maxims burst into life spewing their lethal stream of fire. Every fifth round was loaded as a tracer bullet, incendiary rounds, the pyrotechnic powder burning brightly in the daylight. The sizzling flight paths were clearly delineated against the aquamarine, deep green and brown backgrounds both surrounding and of the targets. He'd hand loaded these himself last spring. The gunfire and engine roar overwhelmed all other sounds, the breeze, birds, the workers' nail guns, the small waves lapping against the boats and rocky shore. The two men on the roof looked up stunned, not believing what their senses were telling them, that death was riding down on them. They never even had time to try and leap from the roof to safety. In seconds the bullets ripped up the dock in a cloud of wood splinters and fragments, then destroyed both watercraft, tore up the ground, the main building's deck, and the center of its roof before sending the two workers into the afterlife. Initiating a sharp bank back towards the direction he came from, he fired a last burst of rounds into the truck and the propane tank. Both exploded, miniature mushroom clouds expanding and climbing well up above the trees. The concussions rocked the Fokker, but the pilot expertly maintained control of the plane as it was bounced through the air. He powered up the crest of the mountain ridges less than two miles distant. Looking behind him he saw the destruction. Two mangled dead men, dock and boats blasted to pieces and the lodge ripped apart and now in flames as the fires spread to the lodge that was clearly going to be an inferno within minutes incinerating what remained of the two bodies. The truck and propane tank no longer existed. Flaming chunks of that debris flung into the forest from the explosions had started small brush fires. He was reminded of a sign he'd seen long ago when a journalist friend in Cocoa Beach obtained press credentials for him so he could watch a shuttle launch at Cape Canaveral. The shuttle launch pad was three miles away from the Press area, but a large yellow and red warning sign stated with what passed for NASA humor, "In case of shuttle ignition explosion be prepared to avoid Volkswagen size pieces of flaming debris."

The pilot laughed. He liked that. "Volkswagen size pieces of debris." He looked at the red, orange and yellow flaming destruction now burning wildly out of control all over the place. A thick, billowing cloud of grey and black smoke rose to the heavens seemingly alive like some dark entity leaving a scene of evil machinations. This was pushed to the northeast by the prevailing summer wind. He laughed again, before taking a pull of brandy from his flask and continuing his steep, climbing gyre that brought him to the rocky saddle of a ridge that defined the drainages. No one was visible on the ground. No trucks, SUVs or cars either. Home free, he believed when he observed nothing but pristine forest below the Fokker. He adjusted his course to take him eastward while continuing the now gradual climb up and over the Nortons and back to where he'd taken off less than three hours earlier.

Mission accomplished.

***

We made the two-mile hike to Dirt's 1972 battered Green Toyota Landcruiser in less than thirty minutes. The Dog lead the way well ahead of us, then he'd stop and look back as if to say "Hurry, boys. I want out of here." The path along the creek we'd just been fishing broke out of the forest here and there and ran through tall-grass meadows filled with Black-eyed Susans. The deep yellow flowers with the brown circular centers stood just above the grass, still green but gone to seed. We didn't have our cell phones with us. I never did and Dirt always left his in whatever rig we were using. He hated any intrusion, especially those of an electronic kind while fishing. When we wanted photos of our exploits I pulled out the miniature Pentax I always carried in one pocket or another. It was perfect for what we wanted. I'd even managed to sell a few shots taken with it to various fly fishing magazines. Reaching the car and unlocking the door, the cab was like an oven from being in the sun this time of day after we parked it in the shade earlier. The Dog didn't care. He hopped onto the bench seat, curled up and buried his head in his paws. Dirt grabbed his phone but before he could dial 911 the thing started ringing if you called the first few bars of the Dead's long ago song Feel Like A Stranger a ring.

"It's Qualls," he said to me. "Yeah Jim, what's the deal?" He listened for a moment then said "We heard gunfire and several explosions. Then saw lots of smoke and finally an old World War I fighter, a biplane, climbing fast just on the other side of Buck's Saddle. That's what I said, a World War I fighter painted yellow and blue with a white dragon on the rear fuselage. I think it was a replica of a Fokker D.VII. Nothing else looks like that particular fighter.

Dirt loved this period of aircraft, had a number of books

on the subject and had painted a couple of scenics with the vintage aircraft sailing through his landscapes. None of these sold, so they hung in his studio along a whitewashed brick wall.

Dirt's phone wasn't on speaker, but I could hear the angry almost mocking tone of Qualls' voice.

"Give me a break. You know that I know a shit load about those planes from that period. Yeah we were fishing the headwaters of Indian Creek, trying to find some cold water and enjoy the day, but now that's shot to hell," he joked. More listening then "Yeah pretty damn good on Yellow Humpies. Some decent fish along the banks in the pockets."

The two had calmed down as they were talking fishing in the middle of all of this.

War had broken out at the Lodge, once called Cottonwood Retreat after the trees lining the creek of the same name, and these two clowns were cracking wise and talking fishing. Biederbeck, Montana. Sometimes life was a level beyond Looney Tunes out here.

"We'll meet you there as soon as possible if Bouchee doesn't drive into a tree or irrigation ditch."

"Hoopy toopy ten four," I said deciding to side with the home team demeanor. "Tell Qualls we'll be there in under two hours and we'll give him all the details then. And as always, thanks for the endorsement of my driving abilities."

I'd never had a ticket or a wreck, so I knew Dirt was merely giving me a little grief in an attempt to slightly lighten the ominous situation and how we felt about all of the violence and destruction. We had no idea what we'd find at the lodge. Destroyed buildings, dead bodies, who the hell knew?

Dirt told Qualls our plans, severed the connection with the O'Keefe County Sheriff and climbed in the passenger side. I always drove whether fishing, bird hunting or screwing around in out-of-the-way places. Despite taking pot shots at my skills behind the wheel, my friend recognized and accepted that he was one of those people who looked at driving as one with no ability in foreign languages looked at Russian. You might learn a few words or navigate a few miles, but progress would be slow, ugly, maybe life threatening, at least the driving part of this weak comparison. I could do a little better, so I manned the wheel. Fifteen miles and 45 minutes later we reached the highway. Thirty minutes more and we turned east on another paved road heading towards the Cottonwood Lake turnoff between scenic downtown Lennox, an old mining-ranching community now home to maybe 14 slap-happy granolas, and Yorkedale gone, well, gone in a Yorkedale crazy kind of way – bar with more than one-hundred elk, mule deer, antelope and whitetail head mounts on the knotty pine walls with a few dozen huge trout mounts mixed in for artistic balance, a damn good restaurant across the dirt main street that offered several comfortable bedrooms restored to around 1918 upstairs, gas station, post office, fly-blown reservoir full of stocked rainbow that knew as much about the call of the wild as a New York subway commuter.

As a side note, the best chili dog we'd ever eaten came from the bar's microwave, a large sausage, plenty of homemade chili and a fresh baked bun. You'd think nuking all of this would be disastrous, but it wasn't. Squirt on some French's mustard and away you go. Slam down a shot of Kessler's and a schooner of Rainier and heaven loomed on the horizon. Or was that a shot of Rainier and a schooner of Kessler's? I looked over at Dirt and he said "Don't ask me any dipshit questions" so I didn't. All the same, we liked Yorkedale and its friendly residents. We liked the place a lot.

A little further on we turned back south headed towards

Cottonwood Lake in the general direction of where we'd
been fishing, Cottonwood Creek flowed over a coppery and
gold streambed. We looked at each and both thought trout,
but I drove on. This was the only way in. The spot we'd left
100 minutes ago was the end of the road, a very rough,
rocky logging road. There was no way to reach Cottonwood
Lake in a vehicle other than retracing out steps and then
looping north, east and finally south to this rutted, dusty
piece of kidney rattling crap we were trying to drive on now.
Dirt kept spilling beer on his pants, shirt and thick, grey
mustache. When a particularly vehement lurch knocked the
thick glass mouth clinking into his teeth he said, "Game
over," and pitched the bottle of Boulder Traditional Ale in
the back with the cooler, fly rods and other stuff.
Fortunately it was empty. We'd bought five dozen cases
(1,440 bottles for those of you keeping score at home) of the
stuff when we passed through Calgary to fish the rivers and
creeks of the foothills near Rocky Mountain House last fall.
Good beer, but after the first 300 bottles in the last months
the thrill was wearing off. Dirt had been lobbying lately for
another fishing trip using the Suburban to haul a "shit load"
of the company's Wombat Cream Ale back. A cutesy name
in my eyes, but all the same damn fine beer. I'd probably
tumble to the idea by early October just as the winter storms
began running down the Canadian Rocky Mountain Front
locking up the rivers in ice and snow making for brutal
fishing conditions and wicked driving. No matter, we'd get
fish, eat and drink well and have a high old time of it.

We angled left on the Cottonwood Lake road. What
used to be a difficult, often scary trek was now smooth as
silk. The new owners had improved not only the section on
their holdings but also the parts that ran through private
and National Forest land. Graded and widened, a 45-
minute trip was cut in half. The Landcruiser climbed up and
along the sides of large, mounded mountains that were

more foothills than anything. We wouldn't be sneaking up on anybody. The rusted out muffler was blarping and growling our progress.

"Needs a new muffler, buddy," I said.

"Got an appointment tomorrow at Crash Auto Body. I have replaced the muffler every three years whether it needs it or not," said Dirt.

"How long's it been?"

"Seven years."

We chugged on. Orange, rusty-barked Ponderosa grew tall and thick, the stately trees giving each other plenty of room to prosper and survey their domains. A bushy grey coyote ran for cover at our approach. Ravens and vultures circled in the sky ahead of us. When we rounded the last lazy curve before the two-mile run into the lodge a towering column of grey smoke dominated the scene rising hundreds of feet before the breeze sheared off the top and pushed it off towards the Missouri Breaks. Closing in we could see lots of blasted and burned debris floating on the lake, parts of the lodge no doubt. A canoe, severed in half, along with large fiber glass chunks of a boat's hull lay submerged near shore, scattered along the rocky beach and adjoining grass or all over what remained of a dock. An outboard motor lay like a grey corpse in a few feet of water a prismatic fuel and oil slick washing onto shore. At the turn down into the lodge a sheriff's pickup was parked, red, blue and white lights flashing. I rolled down the window to speak to the 6-6, 290-pound deputy, George Mitterwald, an old friend of both of ours – a good guy and a honest, diligent, hard-nosed cop who'd seen almost all of what the human race was capable of doing to itself over his decades of service, all of them except for two years in LA working in Biederbeck. He helped gather evidence that led to the arrest of one of our more creative city managers who was making money, lots of money, taking bribes to use his influence to sway the city council to approve horrendous projects from out of state developers. Greedy bastards all of them, a lot like the three murdered on the river in July.

"Hey George. Qualls wants to talk with us," I said. "We saw some things that may be important to what happened here."

"That's what he told me, Ed" said Mitterwald. "Hell of a fine way for the day's fishing to end for you two." Everyone seemed to know what Dirt and I were up to all of the time.

"No shit," Dirt and I said in unison like some lame chorus of some obscure derelict angler's society.

We looked along the lake up to the charred and smoking remains of the lodge. Small fires still burned in the rubble. Shattered and blasted glass reflected the sun's light over a wide area. An old Willys Jeep had been blown on its side and now reclined resting against a large Ponderosa. I spotted Qualls' truck, an ambulance, two squad cars from nearby Harlowton, two fire trucks, a state Highway Patrol cop car and a couple of local pickups, local based on their muddy, banged up condition. We looked on as two body bags were loaded into the ambulance, a somber, grim sight. Mitterwald waved us through. We drove slowly to a level spot not far from the destruction. I parked the Toyota, which dieseled for a bit when I turned the engine off, finally giving up the ghost with a loud backfire that turned everyone's heads until they realized it was just us and Dirt's rig. We got out leaving The Dog on the front seat. He was looking around, sniffing and assessing the situation but showed no desire to leave the safety of his ride. Qualls spotted and walked slowly towards us. As he got closer we saw a look of anger and worry on his face. The anger part we were familiar with. The worry was a first. As if the incinerated lodge and dead bodies hadn't clued us to how bad this was, the sheriff's expression and tight body movements did.

"Look at this bullshit," Qualls said while swinging an arm across the expense of the damage. "Two innocent men gunned down and burned to a crisp. And only some trace evidence."

""We've got real troubles in our country," Dirt said. "Can't ever remember anything this rough happening in the forty years I've lived around here."

The air smelled of charred wood and something else, sickeningly sweet like a family barbecue gone seriously wrong. I stifled my gag reflex and Dirt spit in the dust at his feet. The various vehicles' flashing lights reflected off the depravity and the trees, the colors muted in the harsh light of afternoon. Sounds were muffled too, men working professionally passing information and requests among themselves in low voices as if in respect for the dead and the ugly nature of the crime.

"Awful isn't it," said Qualls. "Never get used to the smell – two men, a dog and a mule deer buck killed by the explosion. Think I'll have the house salad tonight, Dirt."

Cop humor was needed right now to hide personal feelings and move beyond the grotesquerie dominating what was once a seen of serene natural beauty.

Qualls and I nodded in agreement. He was born and raised in Biederbeck. I'd called the town home for close to thirty years. We were all from the same generation, thought alike, listened to the same music, read the same types of books and shared a lot of other things in common. Mitterwald called us The Three Stooges Biederbeck Style. And who said that the Algonquin Roundtable was dead. Murders, robberies, bar fights and the like, while not uncommon. They happened in O'Keefe County like anywhere else. Our beautiful niche in the world was not immune from the often nasty doings of our species. But these two murder scenes, the now five dead and the exceptionally violent nature of the killings, this was something else, beyond our imaginations which to be fair were quite imaginative.

"What evidence," I asked?

Qualls produced a plastic evidence bag containing a handful of brass shell casings.

"Can I see that?"

He handed it to me. I examined the casings. They all had the same PPU stamped on one end and 7.65x53 on the other end - clearly a direct link to the murders on the Yellowstone a month earlier. A week ago Qualls let me in on what the ATF had learned about the casings. Much the same as The Count had told me but not with quite as much detail. The ATF knew their stuff, but so did my friend.

"Well, at least we know that the same bastard who did the three on the river, did this," said Dirt who quickly held up his hands and added, "I know, I know, belaboring the obvious here."

"Obvious but not much closer to finding the person who has murdered five men," said Qualls. "To say these two crimes were not done by the same person would be stretching coincidence into the realm of incredulity.

"We might be able to help on that front, at least get you pointed in some sort of specific direction," I said "And what about the FBI?"

"They're still busy with the Freemen crap and since this happened on private property they're leaving it up to my department," said Qualls. "The state boys will be leaving soon, also. Screw them. When all of these agencies get involved it becomes a law enforcement alphabet soup with everyone tripping over each other's feet. This is my turf and I'll damn well handle it. What did you two see earlier?"

We filled Qualls in on hearing the gunfire and then the explosions and then watching the smoke cloud rising above the ridge far into the sky. Dirt explained about the biplane and how he immediately recognized the type of fighter and the singular paint scheme, that of Wilhelm Leusch who scored five kills and died a few years after the war ended. Qualls didn't question the ID. It was well known around town that Dirt had a fascination with World War I aircraft, one he said began long ago when he saw the 1938 film The Dawn Patrol starring Errol Flynn, David Niven and Basil Rathbone. I'd watched the movie with him countless times in his den. It was okay, and good whiskey and fine cigars definitely helped where I was concerned. Dirt loved the movie and any others relating to the subject including the Blue Max with George Peppard. This one was so bad, I could only watch it once. Its only redeeming factor was Ursula Andress. He'd considered buying a replica of the Nieuport 28 from some collector in California for $225,000 and learning to fly. Since even on a good day driving was a sketchy proposition for the artist, we all convinced him over time to abandon this desire and save his money for something worthwhile like an even better sound system for Ray's. This decision more than likely saved our friend's life and his bank account a lot of money, but on occasion he still raised the specter of a crazed Biederbeck madman flying haphazardly over our skies or crashing in the river.

With our information on the Fokker, Qualls decided to interview anyone he could find on the east side of the mountains about whether the distinctive airplane had been sighted. A story and photo to be provided by Dirt from his extensive archives would be placed in the local paper and over the air with any state TV station that was interested. And what TV news team smiling and yukking it up night after night while passing on the most god awful news wouldn't jump at the chance to air this? Maybe all of this would lead to the killer or killers.

We talked a little more about the mess here and at the river, how the first three victims had been cremated when the remains were released by the state ME and the sparsely attended funerals consisting of family, a very few friends, a handful of curiosity seekers and Mitterwald. The deputy noted everyone present, ran checks on those not already looked at by the FBI, state cops and O'Keefe County office. The search came up empty once again. We parted company, Qualls walking back to the ambulance, us back to town.

As we neared the town limits on a mostly silent drive home, we didn't feel in the mood for talk or music including The Dog who was asleep between us, I mentioned that I might head up to Lester's ranch in the next day or so and see if he'd seen the Fokker or had any ideas.

"Can you make it the day after tomorrow," asked Dirt? "I'll clear my slate and go with you. I want to talk with Lester, too."

"I don't suppose fishing that spring creek enters into the equation," I said not as a question.

"It does," he said.

We parked behind Ray's, already filling for cocktail hour. Drinks, but not any real food seemed like a damn fine idea right about now. Waukonda greeted us as we walked through the kitchen. The latest fiery murders had been all over the news and she could tell by our drawn looks we were well aware of this.

After a couple of bourbons both Dirt and I felt a touch better. I called Lester. The phone rang out and went to voice mail. No answer. I asked if we could come visit the day after tomorrow, the 20th . I mentioned that I'd bring The Dog as he requested on my previous visit, wished him well and hung up. Since tomorrow was looking empty, I asked Waukonda if she wanted to go fishing on the river down by Reed Point. She's in her early forties with deep red hair. Quite athletic, a lover of yoga with a superbly dry, sophisticated sense of humor. She'd say something to me and halfway out the bar on my way home I'd say "Oh," and realize that I'd been had in a friendly fashion. Divorced once from some Texas clown, and a former flight attendant for a large airline, she could fish as well as any of us and outside of Ron Santo, was the best wing shot in town. Neither of them ever missed whether it was windy, wet, cold or the Hungarian and Chukar partridge were flying like lunatic buzz bombs. Didn't mean a thing. They always hit what they swung on to. Grouse and pheasant were too easy for her. Where she learned to shoot or cast a fly for that matter was her secret. She arrived at two with two magnificent Beretta Diana side-by-side shotguns, 12 and 20 gauge, several vintage bamboo fly rods by Paul Young, Heddon, Edwards and Constable along with a couple of dozen Hardy reels and a few Thompsons from long ago West Coast manufacture. When asked about all of this sporting splendor, she smiled demurely, for her anyway, flashed her grey-blue eyes and said I guess I always knew how to do some things the right way and quickly understood that I wanted high quality gear made back when quality meant something to do my bird hunting and fishing. I liked her a lot. She was funny, could listen, liked to read, listened to music I liked and the few times she came over she showed a genuine interest in baseball and my Chicago Cubs. I was a goner and being an individual given to swift realizations, starting to see that I was a little in love with her.

Dirt said to me the other day, "Ed, you're the only bozo in town who can't see that the two of you belong together. Crazy being crazy, you two are a perfect match. Get with the program."

She said "Yes," with enthusiasm and a bright smile offering to pack the picnic saying something about slicing up some of Ray's roast beef for sandwiches, borrowing a few loaner bottles from Dirt's collection of Argentinian wine and packing plenty of calamari for my canine companion whose ears perked up at the word and the way she said it directly to him. I'd meet her here at Ray's around 10 the next morning.

"Put all the food and wine on my tab, Waukonda," I said like a big deal everyone understood I wasn't.

Dirt looked at me and laughed while he shook his head. Then he muttered "Writers. PIs. Hopeless."

I was feeling almost happy now.

As I was walking out into the warm Montana night filled with stars and other galactic wonders my phone rang. Lester. He said he couldn't wait to see The Dog and added that Dirt and I were welcome as well. Day after tomorrow would be fine and be sure to bring our rods. He laughed as he hung up. Now I was feeling happy. Maybe things around here were on the upturn. The Dog was already two blocks ahead waiting at the door to our office slash home. I hurried to catch up.

***

The next day I loaded gear and The Dog, picked up Waukonda at her place, and then the three of us headed out of town for our day out together. The drive to Reed Point along I90 followed the river for the entire 60 miles. We didn't see a raft or drift boat the whole time when normally there'd be a dozen or more scattered along the 60 miles of prime trout water. The first murders and now these had driven most fly fishers and tourists underground or home. Beiderbeck was starting to resemble a ghost town. Even the media was strangely absent. Instead they were swarming over and around Jordan and the Freemen occupation of the abandoned government wildlife survey station. The media did make its predictable, jackal-like appearance at Cottonwood Lake, most of them briefly abandoning that deadbeat nonsense in the northeast corner of our state to make the six hour run down to the most recent homicides. A couple of trucks with satellite dishes were on site. "Live from Montana we're on the spot with more carnage for you viewers," or something along those lines. Somehow Qualls made a bizarre, horrible pair of murders seem like just another bad day in paradise. When the reporters learned that the corpses were long gone and now under examination by the ME in Helena, most of them turned around after filing brief segments via their satellite trucks and raced back to where they'd just come from. Lunacy on parade. Where was Wolf Blitzer when we needed him? I'd heard on the street this morning through the grapevine that didn't have to take a backseat to any news source, that most of the big boys and plenty of the smalls had quickly pulled up stakes in town and at the lodge and driven pell-mell like the herd driven nitwits they were back up to the occupation out somewhere in the heart of nowhere.

By late morning a summer wind had come up, the temperature near 90. Smoke from forest fires raging out of control west of here in Idaho and Washington washed the sky of its crisp blue and turned things eerily dirty white. This was an annual occurrence. Those of us who called the West home dealt with the danger and attendant destruction as best we could. We didn't like them but we got through it one way or another each tinder-dry fire season, a time when some creeks went dry, river levels plummeted and the ground duff of needles and leaves crackled beneath your boots. When we stopped at the campground on the river The Dog hopped out, immediately ran to and fro, nose to the ground, right leg lifted at appropriate times as he surveyed and marked his new surroundings. The air smelled of the smoke from the conflagrations. Looking up river was like seeing the world through a gauze filter - things up close appearing surreal with that strange reality fading away into a wall of smoke after a half mile or less.

We left the food in the Suburban, rigged our rods and struck off to where we intended to fish, a series of side channels with subtle currents that always held large, fat brown and Yellowstone cutthroat trout. The Dog picked up on our movement upstream and was soon loping from side to side on the dirt and gravel ranch road, nose still tight to the ground. He'd be frolicking in the water when we reached our destination. Aside from the smoke it was a gorgeous high summer day. When we cut down to the bank of the river and pushed through tall green turning to warm brown grass kicking up thousands of grasshoppers, legs clacking as they flew, glided and caromed into each other or were swept out over the water on a gust of wind. The trout were waiting and we watched as they chased down the doomed insects, the fish slashing and devouring their prey like marauding freshwater sharks. Our fly pattern selection had been made for us. We would use large Joe's Hoppers, my favorite imitation of the creatures cavorting all around us. The Dog was now plowing through the grass snapping at the grasshoppers like the fish in the river. His teeth making clacking sounds as he chomped down on the bugs. He'd have his fill in minutes. This wasn't his first grasshopper rodeo. He was standing chest deep in the slow water by the gravel bank when we caught up with him. Now the sounds of his thirsty slurpings replaced the noise of his insectivorous feeding frenzy only recently completed.

Waukonda and I laughed at The Dog, the beauty of this day despite the smoke, this wondrous spot and being with each other. This was good. I needed more of this type of life. I'd become too much the cynic and something of a grouch since the murders started. We fished for a couple of hours or so catching cutthroat after fat cutthroat along with a few really big browns on the hopper pattern. Waukonda cast beautifully, the line streaking behind her in a tight loop then shooting forward 50 feet to land delicately on the spot she's selected while making her back cast, a period of at most one second. The fly would float easily on the modest bankside current for a couple of feet before a set of white jaws opened on the surface and engulfed the fake. Then all hell would break loose with the fish leaping, splashing and diving down deep while shaking its head. Brought to hand, Waukonda admired the trout before skillfully releasing the fish, that disappeared into the darkness with a couple of flicks of its thick caudal fin. I admired her and took a number of photos of the action. A couple of times our canine companion would swim out to the struggling trout and try to follow its madcap antics about the side channel. Once the line zipped underneath him and the friction snapped the delicate leader. Realizing what he'd done, The Dog came to shore some feet below us, shook himself and watched our actions with a sincere look of remorse that seemed to say "Sorry, guys. I won't do that again." Waukonda put down her rod, went over to him and rubbed his ears and cooed compliments about his lineage and behavior. He was soon back in the river, though downstream of where we were fishing scrounging for rocks that he brought to the shore in his dripping jaws. In no time he'd accumulated a pile of the stones that looked like a cairn marking our day's activities. He dropped down in the grey sand and looked out upon his world with extreme satisfaction. For now the world was his to enjoy.

The smoke had cleared off somewhat. The sky now appeared a shade of washed out blue and the sun, still high in the west, was yellow-orange, shielded enough in the haze that you could look directly at it without blinking or temporarily blinding yourself. The fishing had been excellent to put things mildly, so we decided to call a halt to the angling proceedings, head back and have our lunch. The Dog, with visions of calamari on his mind, was already running along back down the ranch road well ahead of us, nose tight to the ground with visions of sharp-tailed grouse in his mind. Roast beef sandwiches, kosher dill pickles made by a friend of Dirt's, peach pie, some Malbec wine from a Rio Negro vineyard in Patagonia and, since she loved

Cuban cigars, a couple of La Gloria Cubana Medaille d'Or No. 4s. Not bad for a derelict writer slash PI – a wonderful woman companion, my buddy The Dog in fine form, great fishing and superb food, drink and cigars. I realized that I both wanted and understood that I needed more of this life. Living alone, even with The Dog, made it quite easy to slip into extreme narrow mindedness and that dreaded cynicism. No way I wanted any more of that noise.

The lunch was excellent. The roast beef from one of Lester's prized Pinzgauer's aged perfectly and roasted to medium-rare perfection on homemade sour dough bread with the aioli sauce served with Ray's calamari. Was absurdly good. The rest of the feast was equally good. The Dog devoured about a pound of the sea food, belched and collapsed into instant sleep. We put things away, sat back with our cigars and sipped the Malbec. My kind of life.

"Where do you come up with these," asked Waukonda. "This is absolutely one of the best tasting, most floral scented cigars I've ever had. A girl like me could chain smoke and inhale these little beauties."

"I wouldn't advise it. You'd be dead in a couple of months."

"Kill joy."

"Yeah, I know. Life is to be lived to its fullest and the road of excess leads to the palace of wisdom," I said.

"All very true as long as practiced with a hint of moderation."

"Moderation has not and never will be part of my life," I said. "I'm serious here. I'm either all in or all out. That's how it works for me."

"I saw that in you when we met at the Nighthawk years ago," Waukonda said as she leaned towards me. "To recognize this in yourself puts you way ahead of the self-righteous, delusional nitwits dashing around spouting their twelve step, PC nonsense. But enough of this. Let's go back to being self-indulgent kids."

I agreed. God! It was easy to climb up on a soapbox. A classic example of bullshit calling out bullshit. Waukonda agreed and poured us some more wine.

We then talked of this and that including a place Waukonda knew of where I could pick up a couple of well-seasoned cords of aspen from a logger who frequented Ray's. At only $120 a cord this was a very good deal. Talk inevitably turned to the murders. Understandably that's about all anyone seemed to care about around town these days. An act of violence that was at once intriguing in its arcaneness and horrifying at the same time made for excellent conjecture and gossip. This was the type of event that had staying power and would be discussed down through the years over many a drink at Ray's whether it was ever solved or not. The list of suspects most often considered by the slightly sodden sages at our bar was topped by those who felt that some skinhead paramilitary group did the carnage, followed by a Mexican drug cartel flunky high as a kite on his own wares and finally a way-out pyscho killer from parts unknown operating under the influence of a bizarre, insane world view. Oops! That could include any number of us in town. We were mostly harmless, but there were plenty of the evil variety around. I know I dealt with one last year. Analyze all the way to hell and back, in my eyes a lot of the vicious, horrible stuff boiled down to the simple fact that the darkness lurking in all of us wins out over the good in us far too often. Don't blame the parents, the schools, the economy, the fact that Obama is president or any other of that jive. Good versus evil. That's how it works in the human race. Drug dealing didn't appear to be involved. Serial killers were inhabitants of way-out-there-ville by their nature. As weird as all these murders were, in one basic and important sense they were straight-forward massacres. Killing for a reason, white hot rage.

Basic as it comes. Of the three, I liked the skinheads but I knew they weren't involved. Those dumbasses would have bragged about the killings from one bar to the next and already be in jail. I couldn't see any of these three types buzzing around in a WWI Fokker D.VII biplane fighter, so in my mind that left no one on the radar at this point. We discussed what happened at length, more or less in the order of it occurred. When I finished with a detailed account of my visit with Lester at his ranch and that Dirt and I still planned to visit him tomorrow, Waukonda surprised me.

"Something's not right with that man," she said. "Before you came in and had drinks and dinner with him a few weeks ago, he was talking with Santo, The Count and that goofy electronics guy who's always going off about "The Cloud," whatever that is."

"You mean Dale Long. A bright boy. Mad as a hatter, but a good guy all the same. I visit and fish with him often. Don't bother with the cloud concept, it's not for the faint of heart or the stable among us."

"That's the one. Well anyway, Lester was really worked up, angry and almost yelled when he said something to the effect that those developers had it coming and he'd 'Like to someday shake the hand of whoever blasted them to hell.' Then he went off on some crazy rant about how the Yellowstone rangers killed his brother back in the nineties and that he wasn't done with them yet. The Count managed to turn the direction of the conversation in another direction, those strange cows of his, I think. And that's all I heard on the matter. I had food to serve. And that Cloud Nine guy, what's his name again?"

"Dale Long," I said.

"Yeah, him. He said he'd overheard Lester making the same rants at the Nighthawk a few evenings back. Long said he thought the guy's cheese had slipped off his cracker, that he was nuts. Coming from Long that's saying a lot."

I agreed. As I said, Long was a damn good guy, a lot of fun to be with, but he played one of the deepest left fields of anyone I knew. And THAT was saying a lot.

"The intensity of his anger, he looked borderline insane, scared me," Waukonda said. "I don't know if you two should go up there. Something's not as it seems and you know my intuition about weird stuff is usually spot on."

I started to respond and she held up her hand stopping me and added "One last thing. Dirt says you guys saw some old fighter plane yesterday. One of those two-wing jobs. That little fact never made the news and I understand why. No sense in blowing up a solid lead. Well guess who knows how to fly one of those old clunk planes? Mr. Angry Rancher, John Lester. That's who. The guy's always zipping around in that ancient crop duster of his. If anyone can navigate this part of the world it's that guy. He's knows every creek, coulee, bluff and mountain pass for a hundred miles in any direction. And he seems pissed off enough to kill people.

"Just sayin', you know," and she took a drag on her cigar and a deep hit of wine. She looked at me with what seemed a lot more than concern and she sure as hell wasn't smiling. She was worried, very worried.

I puffed my cigar, finished my wine, refilled our glasses and tried to figure all this out while at the same time allaying Waukonda's fears and turning our day back to Happyville.

""Lester is angry, and rightfully so, about all of the changes in Montana and around his ranch. The damage to one of his spring creeks, the new barbed wire fences and the fence posts spray painted orange or tagged with No Trespassing signs. The longer we live, in my case anyway, the harder it is to accept change to our way of life. We like things to stay the way they've always been. The old Montana was just fine. Leave your out-of-state bullshit changes back where you came from. Some of us react more strongly than others. And his brother's death coupled with those of his parents still seems to be an open wound. Dirt said to me about the man's anger and ravings that the guy was blowing off steam. That all of the outbursts were good for a man who lived alone, worked hard and was hurting. Sort of like a safety valve on a hot water heater. I tend to think Dirt is right."

"To some extent, but there's something dark going on inside the man. You two need to be careful up there tomorrow," said Waukonda. "Screw this. Let's go back to enjoying the day and most importantly, each other. "And, by the way, I'm with you all the way about the old Montana and a lot of other things you believe."

Waukonda was back to being happy and smiling. I realized what was happening between us (Hey, I can have the rare swift realization with the best of them) and unlike in the past when I would run as fast as I could from a relationship, I didn't. I was going with the flow on this one.

Waukonda looked around and started laughing. "Don't forget The Dog."

And how could we? He was rolling on his back, wagging his head from side to side in the dry grass snorting, grunting and growling in obscure pleasure that only a dog can truly understand. He'd need a quick brushing before he climbed into the Suburban. He was covered in dirt, grass and twigs. What a guy.

Our picnic was back on track. After a sunset drive back to town with the first storm clouds we'd seen in weeks swirling around the ranges that guarded Biederbeck making for an intense sunset with electric shades of crimson, orange, yellow, lavender, purple and all sorts of other shades, we watched my Cubs beat the Giants 4-3 on a two-out Kris Bryant homerun in the bottom of the ninth. Waukonda and I cheered and The Dog "Woofed." Just a trio of Bozos enjoying life together. We took a bottle of the Malbec to bed with us. Tomorrow was definitely going to be another day.

***

A wild, rollicking thunderstorm blew through Biederbeck in the early morning hours. Fierce wind, hail, lightning, deafening thunder, torrential rain were all part of one hour minute show. While Waukonda brewed coffee and made sure The Dog had his Blue Mountain deluxe dog food, I checked the weather radar on the internet, back tracking to midnight and watching the darkest green shading all the way to purple indicating precipitation measured in inches not hundredths of an inch. The jet stream looped north long enough to allow a low pressure system moving in from the Pacific Ocean to swing through our part of the world and bring some much needed moisture. While the lightning did start some small fires, the amount of rainfall more than made up for this. Stories indicated, that for now at least, firefighters were rapidly gaining control of the fires in Washington and Idaho. Looking out my office window I saw that everything was still wet from the downpour. The air was clear, crisp, cool and devoid of smoke for the first time since late July. Today was August 20th. After coffee we all walked the few blocks down to the Yellowstone which was running the color of an old-fashioned chocolate malted. Several creeks upstream with large eroding dirt and gravel cut banks must have blown out in the deluge. No fishing for the sports today. The water would clear quickly and be back to its good, old aquamarine self, with maybe a touch of silty white, by tomorrow,

We drove up to the parking lot behind Ray's. Dirt was waiting with a cooler, a couple of fly rod tubes, an ancient, blue REI daypack with fishing gear. He looked eager to get going. I kissed Waukonda goodbye, The Dog nuzzled her leg, she rubbed his ears and we all said "Goodbye. See you soon," meaning maybe later tonight or more likely, tomorrow during cocktail hour at Ray's"

"This is getting downright romantic," Dirt offered.

Waukonda punched him, hard, in the shoulder. I ignored all this and threw his stuff in the back of the Suburban

"Take care of yourselves, all three of you," Waukonda said. "Remember what I said about Lester yesterday. You guys try and behave and have some good clean fun."

"Not bloody likely," said Dirt, ever the diplomat.

She walked into Ray's shaking that red hair that shimmered in the morning sunlight. We piled into the rig, gassed up and headed for Lester's Ranch. For some reason the Door's Strange Days CD was playing. This was more than likely appropriate all things considered.

When we pulled up in front of Lester's place he was sitting on the steps sipping coffee. He waved. A Yamaha ATV in flat black was parked nearby. A high plains stealth bomber and the cowboy's modern version of a horse. We disembarked. The Dog hopped out, ran up to Lester, who gave him some attention, then he started his nose-to-the-ground sniffing routine, but kept looking back at Lester. The hair on his back was up a little, a very uncommon occurrence.

"Glad you two made it," said Lester. "Glad you brought your dog. Miss having one around, but I can't bring myself to getting another since I had to put down my Golden, Zack. Don't know how long I'll be around and the idea of an animal without its master being cared for by others or taken to the animal shelter doesn't sit well with me at all. Can't do something like that. It hurts just to think about it.

"I'm caught up on work around here or at least as much as I ever am. Fixed a line of fence this morning that those damn cows pushed through again. Ought to hold up for a few days at least, 'til they decide they want to move off someplace else. I imagine you two are up for a little fishing and so am I. How about taking on the bass in the pond at the end of Wolf Coulee? Some of those suckers are five pounds if they're an ounce."

We said we were game. After loading the cooler, our fishing gear, a bottle of R&R and some cigars, all of us piled in the Suburban, The Dog in back sitting tight to Dirt. Something didn't feel right about his behavior, but I chalked it up to Waukonda spending the night, the drive up here and so on. We're all creatures of habit and life had been anything but normal since the first murders on the river.

We jostled along the rutted two-track bound for the bass pond a couple of miles away. The mountains in the south and west stood out clearly in the fresh air. The high plains rolled off into oblivion to the north and east. The country was so vast, so beautiful and so powerful the experience of trying to take in all the splendor was overwhelming. When we drove past the earthen storage garage I noticed that the chain and padlock were gone, but the large doors were shut tight and a large metal pry bar was wedged through the big handles bolted on each door. Narrow, treadless tire tracks about eight feet apart with a drag mark in-between led up to the doors. Looking the other direction I could see their trail coming from the landing strip.

Lester saw me looking and said "I've been working at cleaning the place up. A ranch equipment dealer up by Malta expressed an interest in all of the old machinery. I'd met him at a cattle auction a while back and mentioned what I had. He's planning to stop by on his way to Biederbeck next month. I finally quit putting the job off and have been going at it steady. I've cleaned up, lubricated and got the stuff in workable shape, at least most of it. Some pieces are too far gone. Hell, anything I get for all of it is found money. None of it's been used for years. I made enough room with all the cleaning to store an old manure spreader that was sinking into the ground on the far side of the strip. The guy can buy that piece of shit, too. Sorry for that bad pun. A fella tends to get a bit strange living all alone with his thoughts out here."

I saw Dirt eye the bomb shelter-like structure and look at me in the review mirror. His expression was pretty close to a combination of curiosity and suspicion. Out of nowhere The Dog leaped over Dirt and out the passenger window. He rain nose down to the ground right up to the big old wooden doors, then raced back and forth the stub of his tail wiggling in miniature circles. I stopped. Got out and called him.

"Get back here, now. Right now," I yelled. "Come on. I mean it."

I didn't like to raise my voice to The Dog, but he was being hard headed in a way well familiar to those who share their lives with English Springer Spaniels. Fantastic animals but they have a mind of their own sometimes. He came back reluctantly, hopped on Dirt's lap and looked out the back window at the doors. The little guy was acting strangely today. Definitely off his feed. I chalked all of this up to a bad day. I've had a few myself.

"Sorry about that," I said to Lester.

'Hell, that's alright. He probably got a whiff of some sage grouse I cleaned in there the other day. A bit early on the season opener, but tough shit. I had a taste for grouse."

We all understood his reasoning and let the matter pass.

"Looks like the storm missed your place last night," I said.

"It did. The noisy sucker raced by to the south hugging the mountains," said Lester. "One hell of a lot of lightning. Could have used the rain, though."

That's how the weather blows in this country.

Torrential downpours in one place and not a drop only a few miles away.

"Anything big floating on the surface will work on the smallmouths," said Lester getting our minds back on the angling thought track. I thought about the fly pattern I'd use on those big fish, but noticed Dirt looking back with The Dog at the earthen structure. Strange days indeed.

We bounced on down the two-track bound for water I'd fished once before, a spring-fed impoundment surrounded by tall cattails. To reach the fish we'd need to push through the cattails for casting room and stand in the muck and sand in water up to our chests. No problem, it was hot out. This would feel good and be a lot of fun. We continued our slow, bumpy cruise through nowhere.

I hoped that our maniac fighter pilot and his Fokker were somewhere else a long way away.

As we drove in I noticed well off in the distance a metal building much like the one used to house Lester's Grumman AgCat. It appeared to be situated at the end of a long, dead level bench, the land running north-south for maybe a mile. I couldn't make out much because of the shimmer from the heat of the day and the distance. Soon we pulled up on the earthen dam that backed up the water. Dirt and Lester were soon in water over their waists casting poppers, large floating flies that the bass might take for frogs, mice or any other small creature. I brought out the cooler and other stuff. In minutes they were both into big fish that bowed their rods and thrashed the pond's surface with violent head shaking. I joined and experienced similar action that continued for a couple of hours before we called it quits to have lunch and some of our Canadian beers. Over more cold roast beef sandwiches, I could never get enough of these, we laughed and talked about all of the big, strong smallmouths we'd just caught. After eating we passed around the R&R and smoked cigars. I went easy on the whiskey, since I'd be doing the driving back to Biederbeck. I was what you'd call the semi-straight driver. Welcome to Montana.

"John, have you seen a World War I vintage fighter flying around in the last month or so," Dirt asked? "Ed and I saw one, a Fokker D.VII biplane to be exact on the other side of the ridge separating where Ed and I were fishing from the Cottonwood Lake drainage. We believe it, to be precise, the pilot who was responsible for both the first murders on the river and now these two."

"I saw that on cable last night, a wrap up on the Cottonwood killings that seem to be linked to the first ones," Lester said as he sipped his beer. "God-damned crazy around here anymore, or everywhere else for that matter.

"To answer your question, Dirt, no I haven't. The only things I see flying around here are off to the south, commercial jets headed to Bozeman, private jets and prop planes going to the same place or into Biederbeck. Something like you mention would stick out like a sore thumb. A plane like that would be a true blue oddity."

"Okay, but keep your eyes open. This guy is way the fuck out of control and who knows when he'll slaughter some others," said Dirt. "Call Qualls if you see anything or have any ideas."

"I'll do that, who do you two think is doing this?"

"Some whacko living way back in the boonies, maybe even off in the Big Empty," and I pointed in a direction that indicated the extremely sparsely populated country in the northeast beyond Lester's holdings. "The guy is a psychopath and probably only flies at night when he hasn't been out for the two attacks. The fact that no one besides us has spotted his plane tells me that he's flying low, a tree top pilot so to speak..."

"Great song. Love Stephen Stills," Dirt interrupted.

I looked at him with a look of don't side track this and

continued, "He probably uses the coulees and then the canyons, flying low, to make his approach, shoots the hell out of everything, then retraces his steps. Only someone who really knows the country around here could pull this off. If he plays things close to the vest, he might wind up killing a lot more people before this is over with."

"I was thinking the same way myself," said Lester. "If he stayed out over the plains on the first attack and worked his way up and over the Nortons on the second, and was lucky, he could get away unnoticed. The fact that you two happened to be fishing where you were was a fluke, bad luck on his part. If he knows he's been spotted he could very well step up the pace of these attacks."

"What pace," asked Dirt?

"Both assaults took place on the day after a full moon. The first on July 20th and the second on August 19th," said Lester. "I'd look for him to kill again on September 17th unless he gets wind of having been spotted. All the same, he may be the type of man, brazen for sure, to stick with this pattern, if it really is a pattern."

Dirt and I looked at each other, dumfounded. Neither of us or Qualls or anybody else had picked up on this. Before this went any further, The Dog perked his ears, at least as much as those big boys could be perked, and woofed at something on a flat rock about 30 feet from us. A rattlesnake coiled in the sun with its tongue flicking in and out tasting the air and then its tail hissing. Rattlers don't rattle. The sound is something that is full of menace and resembles the sound of a tire puncture.

Kapow. Kapow. Kapow. Dirt and I never saw it coming. Lester had pulled a pistol from under his waistband and blasted the snake into bloody pieces. Startled doesn't quite get it. The Dog was scrunched to the ground under the Suburban

"Damn snakes. I don't know how many dogs, cows, cats

and what not I've lost to the things. Sorry if I frightened you. Instinctive reaction whenever I see one. Used to be the Milk snakes kept them under control, but for some reason they're all gone around here. Maybe those crazy Badgers have cleaned them out," and he pointed the pistol at a mound with a hole the size of a coffee can in it. "Like the surly fella that lives in there. Only seen him come out a couple of times in all these years. Take your foot off if you give the bastard half a chance."

"You're a crack shot, John," said Dirt. "I couldn't pull that off and I'm not bad. How 'bout you, Ed?"

"I couldn't hit the rock."

"Years and years of practice and shooting at those things," said Lester. He handed Dirt the pistol which turned out to be a Beretta Model 1915 semi-automatic

"That was my great grandfathers. He used it in WWI and it's been passed down through the family. Takes 7.65x17SR Browning loads. What do you think, Dirt, enough stopping power for a snake?"

Dirt handled the pistol checking the slide and magazine, aiming it at the wet remains of the snake before handing it back to Lester grip first. "It'll do."

We finished our cigars and beers, had a sip more of R&R and loaded up the rig. We'd had our fill of the bass and the gunfire and dead snake put a damper on an easy going afternoon. The Dog came out from under the Suburban and curled in Dirt's lap. On the way back Dirt asked Lester if he could look at the old machinery in the earthen storage building.

"Why certainly. Take all the time you want," said Lester. "If something grabs your fancy, make an offer. When it comes to the stuff in there at least, I'm an easy man to deal with."

We pulled up to the earth and wood beamed garage, shed, bomb shelter, whatever. The rancher slid the heavy doors open with little effort. He was right. They did roll easily. He flicked on some overhead florescent lights. The two of them walked around the equipment that included the antique manure spreader. I wandered around taking in all of the tools, several old kerosene lamps affixed to the vertical beams, three enormous elk racks and a large fuel storage tank along the back wall, not to mention all of the machinery, old tractors, harrows, and a medium-size combine. The entire space was being used but didn't have a cluttered feel to it. A third of the square footage, maybe 30 by 30 feet at the entrance was empty and swept clean. Lester was an organized, neat rancher, not all that common in an occupation where there were never enough hours in the day to complete all of the ranch work. As a result, many men parked whatever they were done using anywhere it would fit. Not in this place that resembled a showroom for abandoned equipment. You could store a Mack truck in this place. A two-wheel caddy looking like a frame for an ergonomic wheel barrow was resting off to one side of the work bench. The air was cool compared to the heat outside, but without a damp feeling.

"Will you take a hundred bucks for this," asked Dirt meaning the spreader. "It would be a nice piece to clean up and display on the patio out back of the bar. Maybe load it up with dirt and plant a bunch of flowers." Dirt was always the sensitive, artistic one among us.

"It's yours," said Lester who pocketed a 100 dollar bill that appeared as if by magic (I know this prestidigitation routine gets old but what can I say) in Dirt's hand. He walked outside while Lester showed me a dozen sage grouse wings he'd nailed to a beam over his workbench, saying they were from the birds he'd just shot.

"I'll call you before the next time I head up this way to haul the thing back to town."

What Dirt really wanted this for I had no idea. Maybe

he actually was going to turn the spreader into a large planter. On the drive back I brought up the tire tracks and drag mark noting how the width on the spreader was a couple of feet narrow and that I didn't see anything that might have made the drag etching in the ground.

"Closer to three feet and the drag marks are heading out of the structure, not in. The soil is pulled in that direction" said Dirt. "Two paces wide give or take. Those wheel tracks are about the right width to be from the D.VII. Same with the width of the tires. The drag mark fits, too.

"I never wanted to think that Lester was involved in any of this, but I've had an odd feeling ever since this happened that the killings were done by somebody local or someone who lived in the general vicinity," said Dirt. "What we saw today up at his ranch, especially the way he handled that pistol and brought up the day after a full moon pattern, kicked my radar up to full tilt alert. I've learned to listen to those quirky feelings and impressions over the years. Saved my life more than once. Coupled with Waukonda's concern, that woman sees things the rest of us don't, I'm starting to think that the guy is behind all of this death and destruction. And where the hell were his two ranch hands? Work up there doesn't wait on a bass fishing outing. God! I hope they're alright. "

Everything my friend had just stated either mirrored or dovetailed with what I was thinking. Qualls needed to be brought up to speed and right away. I didn't think that there was enough for a search warrant up that way, but the sheriff needed to have our latest information so that he could decide on how to proceed. If you put a gun to my head and asked what I believed, I'd be forced to admit that Lester was involved and that his two ranch hands, Jason Heyward and Ben Zobrist, two guys from around here, men who'd worked on the Lester ranch for years, were either dead or in big trouble.

"All of these murders seem to be boiling down to a case of after eliminating every likely and unlikely suspect and possibility, if after doing all of that, what you're left with, as improbable as it may seem, is most likely the motive, means and the murderer points to Lester. Right now that's how this is tracking for me.

"We need to have a sit down with Qualls at your office when we get back. Something's really not right about this and Lester worries me to death. The way he handled that Beretta was more than fucking spooky. He acted like a killer back at that pond." Dirt snorted and looked out his window across the rolling and broken plains that pushed up to the Nortons.

"Man, I know grief and anger has led to a lot of violence including murder all over the planet, but I'm having a hard time wrapping my head around the notion that Lester is the pilot," I said. I grabbed Dirt's freshly opened beer and took a long hit. Designated driver be damned. "I like the guy a lot, but his behavior today and the way The Dog acted spooked around him from the get go, makes me think that we just spent a few hours fishing, eating and drinking with a stone cold killer. I hope I'm wrong. I really do."

I finished my beer and dropped the bottle on the floor behind the front seat.

"It wouldn't bother me in the least if our suspicions were proved dead wrong, but I'm not wildly optimistic on that front," said Dirt as he reached behind him into the cooler for two more bottles of beer, twisting off the caps and handing me one.

What had Dirt's simple request, a lark actually, to look into the killings gotten us into. I liked the non-murderous side of being a PI, divorces, dead beat bill payers, checking out claims of infidelity. The only other case I'd worked involving a killer nearly got me blown away by a big, dark, nasty son of a bitch. That was a road I'd rather not travel again.

Dirt called Qualls and the cop said he'd meet us at my office around 6 p.m. Then he called Waukonda and told her that neither of us would be in that night, that we had a meeting planned with Qualls that was more than a little bit important. I said "Hi" towards Dirt's phone and I heard her say the same over the speaker option. The braver, newer, electronic world marches on. We stopped talking, lost in our individual ruminations about Lester, the murders, the Fokker fighter, the blasted rattler, full moons, all of it. The Dog was curled up on Dirt's lap. A very subdued, concerned and confused group rolled into Biederbeck a little before dusk, but the world seemed a lot darker than that.

***

Qualls was waiting for us when we pulled up to my place. He was sitting on a wood bench I'd bought to lend an air of gentility to the entrance. Two planters made from an oaken barrel cut in half, filled with compost and hosting red, white and blue Verbana plants flanked each end of the bench. Last night's rain had brought the plants back from summer heat doldrums. Perhaps I had a green thumb.

"Let's get to this, said Dirt as the two men followed me into the office. I fed The Dog and after eating he went into the other room, leaped up on the bed and was fast asleep in seconds. I envied him this ability. I've spent way too many nights tossing and turning with my mind running amuck on all sorts of ideas and problems. Booze and a pill or two never worked.

I passed out Special Exports and we settled in. I knew the Cubs were on the tube, but the game would have to wait for now. Gloomy accurately described the mood in the room.

"Before you begin let me fill you in on what the ME in Helena told me this afternoon," said Qualls. "The dead men are Ben Zobrist and Jason Heyward. ID'd from dental

115

records and a driver's license that survived the fire.'

"Shit," I exclaimed. "They were Lester's hired hands."

"Not for the past two weeks," said Qualls. "I called Hartenstein and he told me Lester had let the men go, telling them that he was 'through with the cattle racket.' That he was in the process of selling off his herd."

"That explains the fact that we didn't see any Angus on the place," I said. "And only a few of the Pinzgauers."

"I checked around and found out that Lester had sold the cattle to a feed lot outside of Lewistown."

"I know the place," said Dirt. "Stinks to high hell in the summer."

"Zobrist and Heyward approached Hartenstein about work either on the ranch above Lester's or working on the lodge at Cottonwood Lake. Those two could do anything from ranch work to carpentry. Hartenstein was still in a bad state of mind about his partners' deaths, but he wanted to finish the work on the lodge and then sell it to an interested buyer from Texas. The two started working last week and had been staying there while they did the various projects.

"I'm off duty for now, give me another beer and one of your cigars," Qualls said as he got up and served himself. All my friends knew where all my goodies were kept, not all that difficult. The refrigerator was below the TV and a pair of 100-cigar humidors rested on top. My large storage humidor held over 1,000 smokes and doubled as an end table for the couch along the back wall.

The sheriff handed beers and cigars to each of us. Once they were burning properly we resumed the conversation. Dirt and I filled Qualls in on all we'd seen and not seen at Lester's place that day, our suspicions and suppositions including the strong feeling we both had that Lester was the murderer.

The day after a full moon resonated with Qualls who remembered that Lester's brother Jim's body had been discovered at his residence in Yellowstone Park at Mammoth the day after the full moon.

"Add this and other connections to the fact that word around town is that Lester's been spouting off about the dead developers and how he's glad someone killed them. That the only bad thing about all this is that Hartenstein wasn't killed too. He became so angry at the hardware store that he drove off some customers and frightened the clerk. Same rant at the Nighthawk and I've heard him at your bar Dirt.

"Circumstantial to be sure, but things are piling up for Lester and not in a good way," said Qualls.

"He's been a live wire to be sure, but I thought he was letting off steam," said Dirt. "I'm pretty damn sure I was wrong on that count. If he killed these men, up to five now, he could be planning to take out more and soon. The connection with the developers and their lodge may be important. We need to find out what other holdings they have around here."

"Mitterwald already checked. They own a high end outfit on the North Fork of the Elk River on the northern edge of the county," said Qualls. "Luxury cabins, lodge and grounds with a good cook and plenty of support staff including three of the best guides in the state, guys who live here year round, and not these carpet baggers who spend a few months in the state then head south when the weather turns before coming back up in late spring. North to south, south to north. Stay in one place and let the locals around here make a living."

This was a personal beef of Qualls. Friends of his, hell, friends of all of ours, that were born and raised in Montana were being edged out by the "transients" as Qualls put things, and as a result hurting for money big time. The large outfitter guiding operations had no interest in the people around here, only in turning a buck. I understood Jim's rant.

"In the fall when they aren't fishing they hunt ruffed grouse and pheasant on leases that they have all up and down the valley. That operation also guides day trips and extended backcountry outings in Yellowstone. It's one of the few outfits that takes care of their people and the land. I can't quite figure Hartenstein and his dead buddies being associated with the operation. They just took over this spring, so I expect things to change and not in a good way. I've had George call the manager and give him a heads up, even suggesting that they shut down until this is solved. The guy said thanks for the warning, but no way they were losing the business. This is high season for them. A variation on the 'thanks but no thanks gambit.'"

"The next full moon is September 16th and that makes the 17th a likely time for the next murders," I added after checking my desk calendar. "If more murders are in the offing."

"In the fucking offing," Dirt sputtered. "I'll bet on it. Jim you need to find a way to arrest Lester. He's the one. I know it. The way he popped that rattlesnake, the look in his eyes after he did it, scared the crap out of me. For a second he was blank, put the 1,000-yard stare to shame. There's no one for miles up that way to notice any weird doings on Lester's part. He said he was working on some old machinery he's selling. That he was in his shop all day. He can come and go in his truck or in that Fokker D.VII with no one being the wiser. Using ground and mountain contours he could have approached the lodge unseen or those three developers in the raft on the river. "

"Ease up there a bit Dirt. The days of riding in over the hill vigilante style are long gone," said Qualls. "We need more to go in to make a solid arrest. We don't want to force Lester to go on the run if he's indeed the one we want. He is more than able to disappear in that country up there and never be heard from again. He could slip across the border and vanish somewhere up north in Canada. Obviously we don't want that. If he did all this, we want him brought to trial. Biederbeck will never be the same if the murderer is not found.

"The county attorney says we don't have enough for a warrant or enough information to arrest anyone. What you gave me today helps, it helps a lot, but I need more. George and I are heading up to the ranch tomorrow to rattle his cage some and look around as much as Lester will let us," and Qualls worked on his beer and puffed his cigar.

"The big problem is that we can't put him at either murder site," said Qualls. "He claims he was dusting crops on Ted Abernathy's land. Abernathy said he hired him to do the work, but at the time of the river killings Abernathy was over in Columbus meeting with his banker. And Dirt just mentioned that Lester claimed to be on his ranch fixing equipment all day during the second murders. Not an iron clad alibi. But prove he's lying. We can't right now. His word is as good as anyone's around here. We need to connect him with that old fighter, the Fokker.

"And according to an FBI profile on the killer, he's a white male in his late thirties or early forties, possibly fifty, doesn't have a criminal record, prone to angry outbursts in public, lives alone and has a dependable income in order to support flying. There are so many licensed pilots around here that narrowing down the list takes time. We're on it, but time is something we haven't got a lot of in this case. And how in God's name can these profilers figure he doesn't have a record and this maybe his first crime? Dead, mutilated bodies all over the place. Hundreds of spent rounds. What would lead a sane person to that conclusion with all this violence? First time my ass. "

"Except for the age, the profile fits Lester," I said.

Heads nodded in agreement.

The air was decidedly smoky blue in the room so I opened a window and clicked on the ceiling fan. Someday when my ship came in I'd buy a fancy air conditioner, one with a remote control. My phone rang. It was an older women we knew and she asked if I'd check out her neighbor who she was convinced was poisoning her Guinea Hens. I told her that I'd be busy for the foreseeable future, but would get back with her when I could. As I hung up I heard her say harshly "Ed Bouchee private investigator. My eye," click. Another client lost. Oh well, what we were involved in took precedence.

"That was Donna Zimmer. She thinks someone's trying to kill her Guinea Fowl."

Eyes rolled. We got back to business.

"What intrigues me in all this is why the killer is using a vintage World War I fighter to do his handy work," said Qualls. "That plane used twin Maxim machine guns that fired 7.65x53mm Argentine ammo, not all that hard to find even these days. If he's mixing in tracer rounds that would explain how the fires at the lodge took off so quickly, and some of the damage on the river. Burn marks on the body parts and raft fabric. And where in the hell would you get an airplane that's almost a century old? You'd have to build it almost from scratch, from the ground up."

"The plans are out there and so are old frames, engines and the rest," said Dirt. "I saw a website where a D.VII was built like this. What parts were needed were machined by the builder. It's a labor of love or craziness. Probably both but it can be done. Lester can fix any machinery that comes his way. And there are a number of really skilled machinists. I know of three on the west coast that built parts for my Thompson fly reels and engine parts for that '49 Ford Sportsman Woody I used to have."

"That was a fine car, Dirt," said Qualls. "Never should have sold that one."

"A woman from La Jolla who buys up my paintings like they were candy bars, fell in love with it and I thought I was in love with her. She got the deal of a lifetime on that one and I didn't even get laid. Shouldn't have sold all of my Paul Young rods to her either. I don't think she even fishes. Brain dead sometimes is all I can say. "

"You're hopeless, buddy," I said having had similar experiences in the romance area myself. Actually all of our little circle of friends could tell tales of similar woe. That's how it is.

"This whole thing is, for lack of a better description, violently eccentric," said Qualls. "The murderer seems like he's locked in some type of time warp. I always figured Lester for an up-to-date guy. His ranch runs like a Swiss watch and he keeps even his old equipment in operating condition. And unlike someone in this room, he has a smart phone."

"That would be me," I said as I slid my eight-year-old flip top cell phone in a desk drawer.

"Yes, that would be you and in a way I'm thankful. If you ever figured out how to use one, we'd be bombarded with all kinds of photos, blogs and other inanities that only you found interesting."

"Thanks for the support, Jim."

"Back to Lester. Using his Grumman would be a dead giveaway and maybe he likes the notion of old style retribution for whatever wrongs he believes he's suffered. And I saw the phone, a fancy one, on the bar next to his drink the other night. George and I are going to pay him a visit in the next day or so, sort of a casual chat and look around. Even if we could obtain a warrant to search the place, which we can't, there's so much land, he could stash that Fokker miles from his home."

Something clicked, an image I'd paid scant attention to at the bass pond.

"While I was unloading our gear and Dirt and Lester were fishing I noticed way off in the east a metal building like the one he stores his Grumman AgCat in. It was at one end of a long, level piece of bench land that was perfect for another airstrip. In the heat shimmer at a distance I'm guessing that the bench is well over a mile, but it was hard to discern much detail. Maybe the Fokker is stored there."

"Anything's possible," said Qualls. "Doesn't Santo have a Piper Cub? We don't need a warrant to fly over the ranch."

"It's a single engine Cessna 182 totally tricked out with every electronic gadget known to man," I said. I opened the desk drawer and withdrew my flip top cell phone. "Excuse the anachronism. I'll call Ron."

While I dialed Santo, Dirt and Qualls went back and forth. "Discern. Anachronism. Where does he get this bullshit? One published novel and a couple of marginally accurate stories on fly fishing and all of a sudden he's Edmund Wilson. Biederbeck's very own renaissance man."

My heart fluttered. It was nice to be appreciated.

"Ron, Bouchee here. We need your help." I filled him in on what we knew and needed.

"Tell him the county will pay for the fuel and his time," said Qualls.

Santo said, "No problem. I want to get this bullshit taken care of and any clear day is a good day to fly. Meet me at 5am at the airport. I'll be ready to go get the son-of-a-bitch."

I passed on Santo's reply. Qualls, Mitterwald and Dirt were all busy tomorrow so I was the obvious choice to fly along. I'd never been in the air with the guy, but what the hey, this was important. I could see it now in O'Keefe County Standard.

Local hack PI and inexperienced pilot dies in plane crash. Investigation reveals that area pilot Ron Santo had less than 30 hours of flying time.

122

And so it goes as Vonnegut said in *Slaughterhouse Five* when death, dying and mortality occurred. He apologized for the book being "so short and jumbled and jangled" and added what I think is quite apropos to our current situation here in O'Keefe County ""There is nothing intelligent to say about a massacre".

We finished up all of this by dissecting the apparent connection between the murders and the developers, which included the fact that they owned not only the Cottonwood Lake Lodge but the ranch on the north adjoining Lester's property. We all agreed that we might be closing in on the killer. Tomorrow's flight with Santo along with Qualls deciding to head up Lester's way sooner rather than later, meaning tomorrow, for a look see with Mitterwald might add a lot to all of this. We ended the discussion and went our own ways, Qualls and Dirt out into the night and me to bed. I fixed a quick peanut butter and orange marmalade sandwich and washed it down with a glass of milk before taking a hot shower and brushing my teeth. I crawled under the covers, The Dog looked up from his side of the bed, groaned and went back to sleep.

I had trouble drifting off to the land of nod. A strong feeling that more killings were on the horizon, probably the day after the next full moon, on September17th at the latest, made closing down this maniac the top priority for all of us. Five dead already. How many more?

***

Dog dreams aren't visual escapades of chasing rabbits or grouse, paws flicking as if in pursuit and accompanied by yips and growls. The dream world of a dog is triggered and driven by smell, that of other animals, plants, the earth, water, whatever is riding the wind. The Dog dreamed this night and the surreal journey was also triggered by scent. The familiar smell of the man snoring next to him, the odor of castor oil and gunpowder, the acrid scent of danger coming from the man he'd been around earlier this afternoon. He was fleeing from the sharp sting of little things biting his rump, back and ears and also trying to draw them with him and away from the leader of his small pack. The odor of formic acid and the pain felt familiar, reminding him of the time he got too close to a hornets' nest while romping in the forest outside of town with his buddy, the man beneath the covers next to him right now. They went everywhere together and the man's scent represented security, fun and loyalty. The Dog in his own way knew he'd do anything to protect his human friend, the integrity of their very close knit pack. In this dream he ran and ran hoping to lose whatever was inflicting these hot, stinging bites. The man was running not far behind off to one side and away from all but a few of the biting things that filled the air with an evil buzz that sounded like it came from hell. He was leaping downed limbs and crashing through the pine duff. They came to a freestone mountain stream and plunged in. The attack, and thus the pain, stopped. The Dog awoke startled and angry. He looked around in the dim light of their bedroom and didn't smell or see his dream threat. He scrunched closer to the man, groaned, put his head down and went back to sleep.

***

Santo was ready to go when I arrived. The Cessna was all white, immaculate with black depictions of a wolverine painted on each side of the rear fuselage. Santo saw me looking at this and said, "Read the opening of **Slade's Glacier** by Robert F. Jones and you'll understand." I left it at that and checked the battery level on my phone and also my .357 to see that it was loaded with six rounds of jacketed hollow core magnums. It was and the phone was fully charged.

Santo completed the pre-flight checks and the engine caught before I'd buckled my harness. Biederbeck's airport, marked along the Interstate with a green sign and a white jet like it was O'Hare International, was perched on a bluff that stood a couple of hundred feet above the Yellowstone Valley and town at an altitude of 4,656 feet above sea level. We were cruising along at 7,500 feet, nearly 3,000 feet lower than the tops of the Norton Mountains. The southern and eastern slopes were illuminated in full relief. The part of the western ridges that I could barely glimpse were draped in deep purple, the snow appearing cobalt blue.

From the air the high plains in the light of a fresh day revealed themselves to be covered in an expanding carpet of rich, orange light highlighted by sharp, purple-black shadows. Darkness gave way to the fullest of colors as cuts in the land, coulees and valleys revealed themselves to the sun that as it rose higher in the sky shone yellow shading to the orange that inevitably devoured the darkness of the previous night. Herds of game were gathered in fields, along creeks and rivers. The large animals – white tail and mule deer, antelope, elk – drifted in and out of sight as the morning mists swirled off the waters and around the game. A seven-point elk stood in brilliant relief beneath the sun's angled rays, then vanished in a curl of fog like a creature from another time.

Santo's take off and flying so far had been impeccable. A few minutes back he'd said over the intercom into my Koss headphones, "Don't sweat it. Ed. I've got over 4,000 hours flying time and 1,000 hours in this one." He looked at me through his aviator shades and nodded. "I take care of this craft like it was a member of my family, if I had one. We'll be over Lester's ranch in less than 45 minutes. I'll come in from the south and east using the Cayuse Hills to hide our approach. I checked my maps and found what I think was the bench land you wanted to see. It's about 1.2 air miles from the bass pond you and Dirt fished yesterday."

"You've got this whole thing nailed tight, Ron." I said.

"Thanks a million. We need to get in close to that metal building."

"Will do. We'll hug the land and make as many passes as you need. Qualls and Mitterwald should be at Lester's by now. They left at dawn and wanted to talk to him before he got up a head of steam. That should keep him occupied. He'll never see us. He may hear the engine, but that's it. It's 2.6 air miles from the house to the pond. Nearly four in total. We should be unobserved from the house."

Like every project Ron took on, he did this one with thoroughness and precision. The warming air created a little chop and we bounced around a bit, but I wasn't worried. It was clear that I was in the hands of a competent pilot. Soon we angled north crossing the river and entering land that was nearly devoid of human habitation. Some stock tanks, windmills, a home or two, some farm machinery and cows. That was it in the thousands of square miles I could see from the Cessna. As the sun rose in the sky our star looked like a nuclear beach ball. The light was intense and already I noticed the herds of game moving in shaded cuts in the land or trees and brush along the river and tributaries. I guessed it wasn't even 6:30am yet.

"6:17," said Ron. "We'll be there in less than 20 minutes." He handed me a pair of Leica 10x42 binoculars. "I love toys," he said. "These are literally brilliant and worth every cent I paid for them."

I had to agree. I focused on a bunch of mule deer running up a coulee shrouded in shade. The glasses pulled the animals right up to me with clarity and definition. This was amazing, top shelf optics on parade.

I looked at Ron and he said "Pretty fucking nice aren't they. I have a friend who has a friend who gets insane deals on these things if you follow my drift. Want a pair?"

"I do."

We continued north but now Ron had the plane less

than 100 feet above the surface and he banked tightly and briefly dropping the Cessna down and into a wide cut between a butte and the Cayuse Hills. A large saline seep, a dead zone of alkali salt brought up from the ground by capillary action brought on in part by a lowering of the water table, passed below us. The spot was dirty white with a rogue clump or two of dead Russian thistle marking the edges.

"We'll sneak in along this dried up creek bed. No one will be the wiser including Lester," said the pilot who was grinning but not in a welcome home manner. Ron looked determined and definitely not a man to cross at this time, all business.

Up ahead the bench and the top of the metal shed loomed. Santo zoomed the Cessna up and over a rise and raced along the bench no more than 100 feet above the ground. A well-tended airstrip came into relief, graded, cleared of any obstructions. The building was plain metal. Patches of rust resembling lichen on volcanic clinker spotted the roof and sides of the old building. A large fuel tank stood on metal stanchions along one side. From this height tire tracks and drag marks were visible leading from the structure or was that hanger, out onto the northern end of the air strip. The sliding metal doors stood open a few feet. A padlock and chain hung from one latch. Something large hid in the shadowy interior that was dimly lit by a grimy window in the north side, the east. The sun was doing its best to help us out. I thought I saw a rectangular fuselage, pair of wings and the suggestion of tan color just behind what looked like a propeller. The Cessna rose and banked sharply before dropping our plane down at a frighteningly low level, 30 feet at most. The land rushed beneath us, sage, juniper trees, patches of prickly pear cactus, outcroppings of that clinker I just mentioned, the orange and buff jagged surfaces a reminder of a more heated, tumultuous past in this country, and now the end of the runway and the building. I trained the glasses on the opening and was able to make out a dark shape of maybe an airplane, what looked like wings and a tail rudder. I didn't see the propeller this time around. Two more passes yielded nothing more. The sliding doors on the other side of the hanger were closed and like the front a chain and padlock hung from one handle. Sure seemed like I'd seen an airplane stored in the shed, maybe a biplane, maybe even the Fokker D.VII we were after, but there was no way to be sure without landing and going inside the building.

"There's something in there," I said and started to suggest we land, take a very fast look and beat cheeks out of there when Santo pointed towards the west. A cloud of dust rose behind something miles off but tracking our way and in one major hurry. "Time to beat a hasty retreat, Ron."

"No shit. We've saw what we came to see."

"Yes we did, but it's still not enough to help Qualls with a warrant. It's no crime to have more than one aircraft. Hell, the thing could be nothing more than a cannibalized Grumman for parts for his crop duster. Without a firm idea we only have suspicions that are almost confirmed. Not much more if anything."

"Is that what you really think, Ed?"

"No. I'd bet my Suburban that Lester's hiding the fighter in that building. We need to get back and wait for Qualls and Mitterwald to call. We'll put our heads together in the cop shop as soon as they return."

We made our escape dropping swiftly below the level of the bench and its airstrip. Sun-warmed air rising up the draw bumped and jostled the little plane. Despite this turbulence, Santo had no trouble retracing our low-level route down the draw and out over the river. We touched down at the airport 20 minutes later. I helped Santo tie things up, then we drove back to town.

One way or the other we needed to pin this down and keep Lester out of the air and in our sites constantly until Qualls had enough to haul the man in.

"Something ugly is going on up there," said Santo. "I feel in my guts that more killings are just around the corner.

So did I.

***

The visit went well with Lester for about five minutes, during the "Hi. Nice to see you. It's gonna be a hot one" preliminary bs common to so many cop questionings. Things went south real fast when Qualls started asking about Lester letting go Heyward and Zobrist prepatory to selling off his cattle. By the time Mitterwald brought up the Fokker fighter, the tone of the rancher was just plain surly.

"Listen goddamnit. If you think I had anything to do with these murders, haul my ass in right fucking now," said Lester. He was apoplectic, face beat red, rigid stance but vibrating noticeably on the balls of his work boot clad feet, his brown weathered hands clenching and unclenching, knuckles white and pupils pinned as he stared at first Qualls, then Lester, then back to the sheriff. I've had enough of the FBI, state cops and assholes pretending to be my friends like Bouchee and Tidrow. And now you two.

The pissed off rancher pulled a phone from his pocket, looked at Qualls then the deputy and said "Do I need to call my lawyer for this bullshit?"

"Take it easy John. We're just following up on everything we can think of no matter how insignificant," said Qualls. "You said that you haven't seen any strange aircraft flying over the air space above your land. Is that correct?"

"The first thing you got right this morning. Did you really think you'd catch me napping as the sun came up. Work me over verbally while I'm half awake. Imbeciles. And while we're at it, Mitterwald stay away from my barn. The cop turned away from the barn and moved to within ten feet of the sheriff.

"Holy shit, the planet is overrun with inbred subnormals. You two take the cake."

"John, your word is good with us and we haven't made an effort to obtain a search warrant for your property," said Qualls. "Please calm down. We only came up this way to ask a few questions and find out if you'd seen anything. You've spent as much time in this country as any man. We thought you might be able to help us out with this mess."

Mitterwald started to say something but Lester yelled "Shut the fuck up and get off my land right now! I'm done with you and everyone else. I feel awful about Heyward and Zobrist. They were good men and I hated to let them go, but my damn cows are beginning to cost more than they're worth. I'm shutting things down and listing the whole shebang. Take the money and start enjoying life, maybe someplace in Mexico. I don't give a rat's ass about those three on the river. They got what they deserved. Period. Now leave."

Qualls noticed a pistol tucked into the right side of the rancher's jeans and gave Mitterwald a quick fade with his eyes that said 'be careful.' The two officers backed up to the country 4x4 and climbed in.

"Unbuckle your gun, George."

"Already did," said the deputy who was now holding the gun level just below the dashboard, index finger on the trigger. "I saw his pistol."

"Be ready. I'll back up to that stock loading platform. We'll turn around there and get the hell back to town. If he tries anything we'll have the rig and the platform for cover."

Qualls executed the maneuver and accelerated down the road kicking up dust and gravel as he sped to the highway. In his rear view mirror he saw Lester race off in the opposite direction in his Dodge Power Wagon, a column of reddish-brown dust in his wake.

"That gave me the willies," said Mitterwald.

"Me, too. I wonder what Ed and Ron turned up."

The radio crackled and a dispatcher relayed Bouchee's message to meet at the station as soon as they got to town. Qualls had Mitterwald shift the meet to the private dining room at Ray's because it was just that, private.

"Looks like we'll find out soon enough," said Qualls who blue lighted their way down the road at over 100 mph.

***

Waukonda met us at the back door and gave me a kiss. She looked happy to see us and worried at the same time.

"How'd it go? Find any old fighter planes."

"Actually I think we did," said Ron, his greying hair sticking up all over the place in the dry breeze, Ray Bans cocked back on his head. He cut quite the dapper figure. "From the tight, dark look inside at 80 miles-per-hour Ed and I believe we saw the death ship in question. Lester's got his Fokker D.VII stashed in a shed on top of bench land four miles from his home."

"We were going to land for a quick walk through but spotted a large trail of dust blowing up on the dirt road heading from the ranch to the hanger, so we split and here we are."

"Take care of this one. I kind of like him," she said to Ron who looked at me and shook his head with a smile that said 'Oh boy. Here we go again." I ignored him and gave her a hug. "Ross and I have fresh roasted Ethiopian Harrar coffee, croissants and some bear claws and cream-filled Bismarcks from Big Sky Baked Goods waiting in the back room. We'll leave you guys alone."

"If this wasn't a world class shitty time around here, I'd think that we're visiting royalty," said Ron.

"We appreciate all this," I said. "Qualls wants this kept as quiet as possible until we decide what to do."

131

On cue the sheriff and deputy pulled up. We all walked into Ray's, hung a right to the private dining room and settled in. The coffee and food smelled great. We helped ourselves with enthusiasm. Stress can make for hungry boys. There were two vases of wildflowers on the banquet along the far wall. Where Waukonda found these is anybody's guess - heat, dry air, lush wildflowers. The wooden blinds were down and the slats three-quarter closed. The overhead chandelier was at about half intensity.

"If things weren't so wicked around here, I'd say that this was a damn nice setting," said Mitterwald. "Where's Dirt?"

"It is a damn fine setting. Fuck Lester. Dirt and the Count are over in Bozeman peddling pictures and delivering a washer and dryer from the Count's shop. Those two are in their chasing a buck mode. I'll fill them in later if there's time."

We told Qualls about the hangar and what looked like an old biplane hiding in the darkness. Qualls and a clearly angry Mitterwald gave us a blow by blow on their "tet e tet" as the deputy put it with Lester. They left nothing out. The bit about the obviously exposed pistol and the rancher's menacing expression said as much as anything about who we all considered the prime, the only, suspect in the killings.

We worked on our pastries and drank coffee. Ross brought two more carafes of the stuff in as Waukonda delivered another load of croissants. Then they both disappeared like they'd never been in the room at all. Dirt must have a class on this now you see it, now you don't stuff.

"We need to bring him in and hold him in a cell," said Santo. "He requires you two to give him the prime once over, verbally I mean, nothing physical just yet."

"We're not Chicago cops here. Whatever the guy deserves we'll play by the rules. We've got nothing on him aside from a bunch of circumstantial evidence and conjecture based on experience, both empirical and cerebral," said Qualls. "You know judge Warren won't issue a warrant on that. He is a hard line constitutionalist even when lives may be at stake. Even a killer's rights are paramount with Warren, and in a way I'm glad that there are still men like him sitting on the bench."

"A good jurist, but getting a bit long in the tooth. What is he, eighty? When's he up for election," I asked.

"Not soon enough to help us with this crap," said Mitterwald who was a bit calmer. Maybe it was the coffee and pastries coupled with the subdued lighting and comfortable surroundings. "I think Warren just turned seventy-nine."

"George as soon as we're done here I want you and another officer, Moryn if he's free. You and Walt can handle any rough stuff if it happens. Head up to Elk River. Round up everyone you find out of the place immediately. Don't worry about anything else. I don't care if the lodge is on fire. Shove them in their rigs and head back to town. Lester's about to go off again. I know it. Guides, guests, Hartenstein, I don't care what line of shit they give you. If they won't come voluntarily, arrest 'em all and we'll sort all of it out later. Better mad than dead. Bring them back here. The town can pay for their food and lodging until they make arrangements to stay someplace safe, away from what I feel is the next target. I know Lester's headed to Elk River and I'm betting it's a lot sooner than the day after a full moon. If anything all of our attention will spur him to take action and finish off what he's started."

"Actually, take two rigs and three deputies," said Qualls after a few seconds of thought. "I'd feel better about things knowing you've got some manpower up there. And blue light it all the way without sirens just in case the bastard is driving over that way, which I doubt. He's addicted to his perverse Red Baron fighter pilot notion. He's beyond delusional or sociopathic. He's a flaming psychopath all the way."

"Waukonda said about the same thing to me yesterday and I agree," I said. "This wacko version of his brother's death he's clinging to, blaming the Park Service and still believing that the body's undiscovered. That bothered me a lot when Dirt first clued me in to the real story. I think Lester's gone around the bend."

"Cheese has slipped off his cracker," said Ron. "Just out of idle curiosity, how many officers do you have these days," asked Santo? "I know you can always use more, but what do we have around here, a couple of dozen?"

"Counting George and myself, and it seems like we're on the job 24/7, 22 plus three dispatchers making three shifts of seven and two other officers to help with the rotations. Our budget won't..."

Before the sheriff could finish his hand held cop radio went off.

"Jim we got a 911 from Elk River Lodge. All hell's breaking lose up there," said Dolly Vardon, the dispatcher on duty right now. "They say they're under attack from an old airplane that's shooting at them. That there are dead and injured. I dispatched ambulances from here and White Sulphur Springs. White Sulphur officers are on their way, but it will take them at least 30 minutes. Can you hear any of this?"

The sounds of gunfire, screaming and a loud engine roaring in the background were clear enough for all of us in the room.

"Send every officer on duty right now in town up there and call in everyone else to work the town and hold the fort. George and I are on our way. And keep us posted, Dolly."

"Got it," and the transmission ended with another burst of gunfire crackling through the electronic airwaves.

The two rushed for the 4x4. On the way out Qualls

turned back and shouted "You two stay put. No civilians involved from here on out. I'll update you when I can." Car doors opened and slammed shut, then the O'Keefe County Chevy Silverado screeched out of sight.

I looked at Santo. He looked back. Stay put? Fat chance. We headed for the airport like demon death was on our tails.

***

This place was a sweet setup. The wind moaned through the pines while a river filled with big, fat trout burbled below. The only signs of humans were those fishing a deep run a stone's throw from a century-old collection of buildings that had acquired the reputation of being part of the most expensive fly fishing lodges in North America. The price tag was as much a draw to a certain type of individual as were the setting and the amenities which were spectacularly beautiful and sumptuous.

Owner Twiggy Hartenstein watched from the deck of the large log building that had been restored and brought up to contemporary speed. His angling and bird hunting clients demanded the best including gourmet meals, high-speed internet connections, television, deluxe bathrooms, top shelf liquor, the works. They had a right to demand the best. The prices for staying at the place were outrageous. Hartenstein and his late partners counted on the obscenely wealthy mooches who did not care what things cost. Actually the higher the expenses, the higher their perceived self-worth as humans. These insecure creatures demanded only that they be treated like royalty and that all accommodations and services were the best. New money trying hopelessly to be old money. These lame souls didn't have what it took genetically to make the old-line wealth grade, but to be fair, they sure tried like hell to be something they never could be. It just wasn't in the cards this time around. They were the type of people who always competed over having the most and costliest of everything – Ferraris, Garrison fly rods, 120-year-old-old Hardy Bougle reels, wildly over-priced French wines, destination trips all over the world at the hundreds of places like this one that made a killing playing on this insecurity and that they lorded over each other, not to mention the married ones that displayed trophy wives that were much younger than they were with IQs barely reaching three digits. Their poorly bred children continued the pathetic lineages. The fact that few of this herd knew much of anything about fly fishing especially its history and heritage, couldn't read water or tie a fly to save their lives meant nothing. They were comfortable in their puerile delusions. Hartenstein's operations catered to their every need and whim. Return business and word of mouth recommendations depended upon this well-informed, expensive servility.

The hustler watched as two clients, one from LA and the other hailing from Huntington Beach, cast dry fly patterns to feeding Westslope cutthroat and brown trout in the Elk River. The mayfly hatch was on and the wild trout were rising regularly to the graceful emergence of these delicate insects and sometimes to a fake cast by the out of state anglers. They missed many, but still caught enough to make them think they were real swell sports. There was a constant loud back and forth between the two about bad casts, great casts, fish slipping the hook. They had the Southern California pseudo-hip act down cold. Yeah they knew who the Ford Brothers were, and they'd each owned Austin Healey 3000s and Triumph Bonnevilles in their early twenties when they'd even had long hair and listened to Arthur Lee. But like so many of their kind, they were only committed to themselves. They had no cause or ennobling purpose in life. Only things mattered, the more costly the better; and people were nothing more than variations on the things theme. The fishermen's racket sounded like an inner city one on one basketball game. This type of sideways nitpicking and competition is what passed for joy in their one-dimensional lives. At the end of the day strong drink and rich food would complete the picture of pricey self-indulgence. The lodge's two guides were down in Biederbeck picking up fishing supplies, more booze and some high-ticket food items. Today was a free day of sorts for the two men in the stream. At more than $2,500 a day they could do whatever they damned pleased at any hour of the day as far as Hartenstein was concerned. They could watch sports or even porno on the 84-inch wide screen TV for all he cared. If they wanted female companionship, he'd provide that, at a price of course. He played the phony hail and well met sporting host with a panache that translated to believability.

While Hartenstein watched as the loud pair tried to outdo each other with their angling expertise, the sound of a gasoline engine reached his ears, growing louder by the second. This was no SUV or even an unmuffled tractor coming down the lane. This sounded sinister to the entrepreneur's ears. He walked to the east end of the deck and spotted an airplane angling down to the ground in their direction. It was a biplane. As the craft banked sharply towards the river he saw the tan and blue fuselage and the wings painted sky blue on the lower surfaces and in a mottled version of the fuselage colors on the tops. A large white dragon was clearly visible near the tail. He could also see twin machineguns mounted on top of the engine and a pilot wearing goggles and what looked like a leather helmet.

"God-damn," he said aloud. "It's that fucking lunatic in the World War I fighter." Like everyone else in the state and beyond he'd been tracking the story of the brutal and weird murders in O'Keefe County. The story still played well in the eyes of the media though ran a somewhat distant second to the lunacy up by Jordan.

Before he could warn the men in the river and run for cover, two streams of bullets marked with tracer rounds ripped their way up the moss and grass covered earth and into the deck and then tearing up Hartenstein. As he died the last thing he saw was the plane banking sharply to the right and zeroing in on his clients. He said one last word, "Shit," and died.

The two in the stream looked up at their bloody host as his mangled body crumpled to the deck. His head, nearly severed at the neck, bounced on the railing and came loose from the body, hitting the planking with a thump like a not quite ripe musk melon before rolling under a chaise lounge a few feet away. They tried to scramble out of the stream and into the slight protection of the pine and cottonwood trees lining the water. Wearing waders and battling the resistance of the river's strong current they barely covered six feet before bullets tore up stream and into the men. They never had a chance to look at each other or say anything. Arms dismembered, heads smashed, rib cages shattered, waders punctured, they died in seconds. The Fokker D.VII roared overhead at less than 50 feet, cleared the lodge by the length of a tall bar stool, fixed wheels brushing the tops of a couple of spruce trees sending a bunch of pine cones raining down on the roof and deck, the sound drowned out by the un-muffled engine of the fighter. The pilot aimed for the resort's landing strip where the pilot focused his fire on a Beechcraft Baron that was instantly transformed into flaming junk as if by lethal magic. The pilot zoomed overhead and looked back as the fuel tanks ignited sending a fireball exploding into the blue sky. Pieces of wing, tail and fuselage rocketed high in the air before crashing back to earth mangled, burned, ruined.

"My trademark," the pilot thought. "Fireballs in the Montana Big Sky and ripped up rich assholes."

He yelled and laughed with a deadly growling sound as

he guided the Fokker onto the strip bouncing along the paved runway as he did so and stopping at the near end. The pilot throttled down and jumped out. The plane vibrated and rattled but stayed put. The engine sounded like a swarm of angry hornets whose deep buzzing alternated between loud and menacingly low pitched. He walked deliberately along the gravel path that led to the lodge deck pushing the goggles back on his helmet. He examined what was left of Hartenstein "Turn a buck on this," he said as he pulled a Beretta 1915 Semi-automatic pistol from a holster on his belt, kicked the lounge aside and fired two rounds into the man's severed head. Brain matter and bone fragments mixed with blood sprayed the wooden deck and windows.

The sound of another man's voice yelling frantically "We're being shot by a man in an old plane. He's landed. He's right outside. He's shooting everybody. Oh God! Help me," came from inside, from the large modern kitchen. The pilot pushed open a sliding screen door, walked through the dining room, leather boots clunking on the distressed and very expensive wood flooring and into the kitchen that was well lit, well equipped and large enough to feed a platoon of yuppies and their spawn. The chef was clutching a phone in one hand, a large boning knife in the other, a couple racks of lamb lay on the cutting board. The chef's eyes bulged with dread and terror.. Spittle dripped down his chin. The pilot laughed when he saw that the man had wet himself. He raised the Beretta and aimed at the chef's head.

"Here's is your bonus for working with these assholes."

He put two bullets in the front of the man's skull. Tanned skin and brown hair attached to pieces of torn scalp splatted against the stainless steel door of a Meneghini La Cambusa refrigerator, leaving greasy, red streaks as they slid down the doors of the forty-thousand dollar plus appliance. The body dropped to the floor like a switch had been turned off. Blood pooled slowly on the tiled floor. The heart no longer pumped. The crimson bodily fluid drained at a leisurely pace. After spitting on the dead man the pilot retraced his steps. Outside he saw that the two fly fishermen's bodies were now tangled in a sweeper, a large pine limb hanging out over the river and bobbing in and out of the current, the corpses rising above the surface and then dipping beneath the water in a gruesome parody of life. Trails of blood and flesh swirled on their way downstream where they would eventually merge with the Yellowstone. The pilot knew this as he knew where every river flowed around here. He delighted in the perverse symmetry of the deaths and the body parts and fluids possibly mingling together far downstream all the way to the Gulf of Mexico.

"You'll be joining the remains of three others of your kind.".

The pilot turned and walked back to the Fokker that had turned nearly 180 degrees from engine vibration and torque in his absence, as if the aircraft were preparing for the killer's return and ensuing take off. The pilot holstered the pistol, climbed in, took a deep drink from a silver flask, throttled up and within a few hundred feet he pulled the Fokker into the sky. He banked hard left and homed in on the main building and its two dead men. He fired the last of his rounds shattering windows and wooden shingles as he flew overhead. Glass shards and wood fragments cartwheeled in the sunlight. The pilot noticed this and said "Beautiful," as he took another swig of brandy before stowing the flask in his coat. The pricey sportsman operation was in ruins, but this time not in flames. He'd missed the propane tank and gas lines coming into the structure and the tracers failed to ignite the logs. The pilot didn't care. He'd accomplished his mission which was to kill Hartenstein, shoot up anyone else present along with the main building. So even though the tony lodge was merely shot to hell, he felt good. The Beechcraft, an unexpected bonus, was still flaming and smoking as he set his sights to the east and the airstrip on his ranch less than an hour away. The castor fumes blowing back from the engine reminded him of this killing, the slaughters. He drank in the smell. He liked to be reminded of this death. Still, he had more work to do this day, much more.

***

We were in the air within 20 minutes of leaving Ray's. Once up, Santo struck a direct course for Lester's remote airstrip. No stealth this time. The early afternoon air was warming rapidly and the small plane bounced up and down like a little kid on a trampoline. I checked to see if my pistol was loaded. It was. My phone had a full charge also. I was ready for whatever came our way. If only I'd known what was waiting for us up at Lester's.

"We're coming straight in whether Lester's there or not," said Santo. "As soon as we check out the situation, call Qualls and update him, providing our rancher friend isn't home. I'll keep the plane running and ready to lift off in case things turn hairy in a hurry. If there's time, check out the inside of that hanger. God only knows what that asshole has in there. Guns, maps, explosives, sex toys, your guess is as good as mine."

"Sounds like a plan. At least as much of one as were able to come up with on such crazy short notice. I always figured him for a good guy, but I was obviously very fucking wrong. He's batshit crazy and a murderous clown."

"I've got my Sig Sauer under the seat and my phone's right next to it," said Ron as he lit a Camel straight in a mildly amazing display of dexterity considering the turbulence. "Helps even things out, soften the rough edges," he said through a thick exhaled cloud of blue-grey smoke. "With my 16 rounds and your six we might be able to hit the bastard if we have to.

141

"Or if I fucking want to," my friend muttered.

The air was hazy with late summer heat and the dust scooped up from the bone dry earth of the high plains from the summer wind but I had no trouble making out the strip and hanger in the distance. The afternoon vibrated with an ominous frequency. I felt that there was danger at the door as they say. My nerves and senses were keyed up, pinned on high alert. Santo glanced over and laughed.

"Haven't seen eyes like that since I did Raggedy Ann blotter acid in college and made the mistake of looking at myself in the mirror. Obviously we're locked and loaded."

"I did some of that very stuff at a Finchley Boys concert at Lake Forest a long time ago. Those boys were strange to begin with. The acid just kicked things into another dimension," I said while digging out my Wayfarer sunglasses and hiding my eyes. I was more often than not a very private, undercover kind of guy.

"Great band. The boys were way out there especially the red-haired singer with the boa constrictor. And the guitarist with the fuzzy hair he grew over his eyes then cut out two peep holes and painted blue frame glasses around the entire concoction. Everlasting Tributes and the oh-so-fucking-rare Practice Sessions. Admittedly not as hip as N' Sync, especially those idiots' Home For Christmas album. That kind of dreck doesn't just wander down the pike any old day. But yeah, the Finchley Boys were a band made in heaven for well-healed acid freaks."

We both laughed and then turned silent as we neared the landing area. Wired. Full-tilt radar on maximum. So wired the world looked more than crystal clear with objects in crisp view yet vibrating subtly with that Finchley Boys acid clarity. Hadn't felt like this, seen the world this way, since doing a whole lot of psilocybin while fishing the Elk River in British Columbia for westslope cutthroat and enormous bull trout 35 years ago. I loved the high, the expanded vision, just not what Ron and I were going through to get there. But to borrow from my nut house friend one last time on this deadly crazy adventure, "Hoopy-toopy ten-four."

"Focus, asshole. Focus. Down. There we go," said Santo who angled the plane about ten degrees into the crosswind before kicking the rudder in the opposite direction to the wind to line up for the landing a few feet above the ground. as we zoomed in and rolled up to the hanger in seconds. A hell of a landing considering the wind and the high anxiety situation we just flew into out here in the sand blasted heat of this piece of big empty lunacy. Rattlesnakes, sage brush, vultures, coyotes, mule deer, prickly pear and maybe Lester in his looney tunes fighter plane any time now. No shit. This was my idea of enjoying myself in Big Sky Country or was it The Last best Place. We had Bud Guthrie and Lonesome Bill Kittredge to thank for those hideous appellations concerning our home. Thanks boys. I really mean that. Thanks a lot. I realized that what was left of my little pea brain was running badly all over a chaotic cerebral landscape because I was afraid and loaded with adrenalin.

I'd been shot at a few times. Never hit. Loggers, gold mine guard, a pissed off girlfriend. The average stuff most of us experience on a routine basis. Once I even fired on a drunk wife beater as he fired at me, but only managed to hit the son-of-a-bitch in the right thigh, though the jacketed magnum round tore bloody hell out of the muscles. Hapless bastard walks with a crooked leg, a cane and a healthy limp these days. Hell, great distances were involved. Upwards of 14 feet. It looked like a scene out of Hearts of the West. Clearly I'm no marksman.

Except for the sound of the wind whipping through the sparse ground cover, along the dry ground and whining through the metal walls of the hanger everything appeared peaceful non-threatening and quiet. The land was burned a parched end-of-the-year brown and grey and tan and bleached out green. The sky was a washed out blue that looked more white hot then anything. The air smelled of Saharan daydreams and the sweet slightly acrid smell of sage cooking under a withering sun. No birds, mammals or silent reptiles in sight. A dead day full of unseen malevolent life. This landscape made Eastwood's spaghetti western locations seem tropical. But fortunately so far, Lester and his vintage Fokker were just not around. I jumped out and ran into the hanger. The darkness of the building was ripped by sharp shafts of glaring sunlight knifing through the blackness through the door openings, front and back, and forcing its way past the spider web and dust choked windows turning the afternoon radiance a spectral and dingy moon glow. The place smelled of cordite, high-test fuel and desolation. I could hear the weathered orange windsock whipping in the southwest blow. The day, this horrible feeling place like death, misery and abject sorrow were in control here reminded me of some external scenes of Val Kilmer's movie Salton Sea. Grim. Awful. Disheartening. On a workbench hundreds of rounds of ammunition were scattered about. A bunch crunched beneath my boots on the concrete floor. I picked up a shell and examined it in a crease of light. 7.65 x 53mm. "Shit." No doubt now, as if there still remained any. Lester's our killer for sure. To my right on the bench I spotted a medium-scale topo map of the this part of Montana spread out and held down flat with jars of washers, nuts and bolts. Scanning the thing in the dimness I was still able see that Lester had marked with vector arrows in red ink along with dates at the site of the first killings on the Yellowstone – July 20, at Cottonwood Lake – August 19, at a location on the North Fork of the Elk River - September 17 and with a circle around the airstrip at Mammoth Hot Springs in Yellowstone Park – October 17. No doubt indicating the day after a full moon on the specific month for each attack. A leather-bound notebook rested next to the Mammoth map site. It was open to a page mildly yellowed with age that read simply and terrifyingly, "Damn the schedule. Slaves to timelines are imbeciles. Bouchee, Qualls and the rest of them are finally on to me. Real sharp minds at work there. High time to finish what I set out to do all those years ago. Kill the greedy, self-entitled bastards. Elk River Lodge and its California rich scum. And then Mammoth Hot Springs to even things out a little for Jim's death. Lots of sheep up there. Many will die today – September 2016 – A new moon will have to do." I looked at my watch. The mad man had lost track of the days. Still August around these parts. What difference did a date make. Killing is killing and Lester had a taste for bloody murder and he was damn good at it in his airplane. The bastard had already murdered at least nine men now including those up at Elk River Lodge.

I ran outside and screamed at Santo to be heard over the plane's idling engine, "There's a map with locations and dates and a note that today is the big finish. He plans to kill as many as he can. He's headed for Mammoth Hot Springs next. This afternoon. Call Qualls and alert him. I'll call Park Headquarters and warn them."

Santo saw the urgency in my face and pushed a couple of buttons to call Qualls. I did the same for Mammoth. I had the number saved because I was always bothering the rangers up there about the current water conditions and any fishing reports they may have. The park boys humored me, had great info and even went fishing with me a few times on the Yellowstone, the Gardner, the Lamar and Slough Creek. Wonderful streams all and good guys. I hoped they'd take me seriously on this Lester business and be up to the task of protecting human life and dealing with that crazy fucker in the old fighter.

I got the receptionist at headquarters and said in a loud

voice that I need to talk to anyone in charge or nearly so, that murder was flying the Park's way.

When the guy asked what I meant, I explained that it related directly to the killings on the Yellowstone and those at Cottonwood Lake. That I was Ed Bouchee and was helping Qualls and others with the investigation. He passed me on with a series of clicks and buzzes.

The next guy, Derek Trucks, wasn't someone I knew, but he was familiar with my act.

"What the hell are you up to, Bouchee?" he asked in an aggravated voice. Another end of the summer burned out Park Service employee. The poor souls see every kind of stupid, criminal and moronic behavior in the space of six months year after year. Babies posed in moose antlers. Arms around bull elk, trying to wade the Yellowstone below the falls, walking up to grizzlies and the usual human stuff like robbery, rape, spousal abuse and even murder at the campgrounds which like the one at Madison Junction were miniature cities populated with an eccentric crew of yahoos from all over the world. I loved the Park in summer.

I calmly explained what we'd found up here, what Qualls was doing at the latest crime scene and that they'd better clear the Mammoth area and prepare for a lunatic in a WWI biplane fighter in blue and gold with a silver dragon painted on its tail flying in and raking the place with 1,000 rounds of gunfire.

"This is real. Absolutely insane but totally real. It's happening right now," I said calmly but firmly. "Do what you can do and do it fast. You may have less than an hour."

To his credit, the head ranger I learned later, took me seriously, said he would do what he could and hung up. I could imaging the frantic alerts and radio chatter among the rangers, bull horns ordering a few thousand tourists to get the hell out of Dodge and all of the Park Service guys arming themselves and preparing for something they'd never in their wildest thoughts had ever imagined might happen and happen pretty damn soon. I hear Ron finish off his call to Qualls.

"Qualls is on his way with reinforcements and he's calling every cop in the area to code 3 to the Park and also coordinating with Park Headquarters," said Santo. "Some ranger named Trucks. He tried to sound angry that we'd come back, but I could tell he appreciated the shit out of our information. Now what? I say we beat cheeks to Mammoth. Maybe we can help out."

"I just spoke with Trucks. He's on board with this. I'm with you," I said, "Maybe we can force him out of the air space up there or what the hell, ram him in mid-flight. We can't live forever."

Ron grinned and shouted with two thumbs up, "Always wanted to go out in a bizarre blaze of glory even if its connected with weird shit like this."

I started to climb into the cockpit when a dark spot far out beyond the southern end of the runway caught my eye. Even at this distance in the burned out sky I could make out the twin wings of Lester's Fokker D. VII. The sound of the engine came to me on the southwest breeze, for now just audible over Ron's Cessna, but growing in volume and rising in pitch – a mean, deadly sound. Now I could make out the all too familiar color scheme and then the dragon as Lester approached the strip crabbing the plane more than 20 degrees into the increasing force of the wind.

"I pointed and yelled, "Lester."

Ron looked over his right shoulder, turned to me and shouted, "Take cover in the hanger. Use the .357 if he comes in range. No questions. Shoot the fucker."

"What are you going to do?"

"Leave that to me." With that Ron motioned me away with his left arm. As he did so light bounced off his gold watch. Even in the manic moment I noticed that he was wearing a Vacheron Constantin Metiers D'art Tribute To Great Explorers Christopher Columbus Expedition watch. I'd just done an article for a magazine on the most expensive tools, embellishments and affectations an outdoorsman could find. This watch was one of the items. No mistaking the maps on the face. No getting around the $110,000 price tag either. I realize now, when it may be too late, that there was a lot of fascinating stuff spinning around my friend that I knew nothing about. Hopefully we'd be given the chance from the powers that be to learn more about each other after this carnage was over. Ron turned back to the controls and spun the plane around with a nifty use of flaps, breaks and prop until the Cessna was now facing Lester who was nearing the end of the landing area less than 50 feet above the ground.

I ran to the hanger and took up a position on the edge of the door nearest Lester. I was shielded but could see everything by leaning slightly outside. I assumed the rancher had spotted our plane but based on the fact he was about to touch down, didn't give a shit. He just kept coming on, the Fokker growing steadily in size, definition, sound and perceived malevolence. Ron revved his engine to a high-pitched whine, the noise sounding like a very angry and very large wasp. The wind was really angry now, sending intermittent sheets of dust and clumps of tumbleweed whirling across the crushed stone, gravel and dirt runway. A trio of dust devils spun madly along the eastern edge of the strip sucking up and shooting any plants not firmly anchored in the ground hundreds of feet in the sky. Then they formed up into a miniature tornado that tracked haphazardly northeastward like a Rush Street drunk. The thing was making a piercing hissing sound in the process. I watched as a coyote was vacuumed off the prairie floor and sent spiraling upwards then expelled horizontally out of the maelstrom and out over the bench land. The last I saw of the bewildered canine was the creature wind milling its legs, tongue protruding from toothy jaws, as its body tumbled out of view. The tornado followed the animal spinning a path down the coulee. Soon all I could see was the widening gyre-like top of the whirlwind that coursed down slope and quickly out of my vision. I followed its course by observing tumble weed shooting above the edge of the bench like chunky smoke from a huge locomotive. To call this scene with all the craziness that was linking together out here surreal was a major example of understatement.

What the hell was Ron thinking? Did the guy have a plan? Was he really intending to go out in a suicidal burst of glorious mayhem? - a high plains aeronautical head on demolition derby. God, I hope not. That probably meant death for sure for both pilots. Lester deserved to die. Ron did not. I was now reduced to the role of horrified yet fascinated spectator. I saw my friend set his pistol down beside him, adjust his glasses, stick an unlighted Camel between his lips, tighten his safety harness and turn the Cessna loose just as Lester cruised over the airstrip only feet above the ground.

The Fokker maintained its speed, over 60 mph, after its wheel contacted the ground. Santo's Cessna rapidly approached rotation speed as the little craft zipped down the run way straight for Lester. The two planes were less than a pair of football fields apart. Neither was giving an inch and neither showed any inclination to avoid a crash by taking off. I stepped out in the open, the wind rocking me with its force, The Cessna and Fokker fought the gale, closing fast on each other. I pulled my Smith & Wesson from the back of my jeans for no good reason and started running after Ron. Then I halted and watched what seemed inevitable, the death of my friend and that of Lester. The Fokker and the Cessna powered into each other, a direct hit at a combined speed of more than 120 miles-per-hour. Lester's plane exploded and was engulfed in orange, silver and blue flame. Shattered chunks of the prop, wings, fuselage and motor exploded everywhere like the machine had taken a direct hit from a bazooka. What remained intact careered off the east side of the strip and down the gulch. The last I saw was Lester's arms and head blazing in flame.

Simultaneously, or nearly so, I watched the Cessna disintegrate in to a thousand pieces, some as big as large pumpkins, some much smaller and one that looked like the part of the wing soaring downwind like a traumatized surf board. As the craft came violently apart I saw Ron being catapulted from the wreckage. His body still mostly strapped to his seat like he'd been shot from a cannon, an arm and leg flapping loosely. His body and the seat cartwheeled to the opposite side of the runway, arcing maybe 20 feet up before crashing to earth on the edge of a wide ditch covered in a clump of juniper bushes, a wild circular hedge-like grouping perhaps 30 feet in diameter. He disappeared in the center of the bushes. Fortunately the wind overrode the sound of Ron's vicious landing.

I raced to my friend certain that all I'd find would be his fractured, mangled, bloody remains. I called Qualls as I ran and shouted, "Ron's plane exploded. He's badly injured. Get fucking help here now." I dropped the phone as I reached the junipers, their gin-like scent thick, even in the wind. I'd pitched the pistol many yards back.

There he was still connected to the seat, now perched at an angle that made him look like he was in a recliner watching an addled nature show on television. The shredded remains of the Camel clenched between his teeth. Ron's shirt and pants were soaked in blood. A gash ran from one side of his forehead to the other and was bleeding profusely. The arm and leg I'd watched waving freely during the brief flight were in bad shape. The right leg had a compound fracture below the knee. I could see ragged off-white bone ends sticking through torn flesh and clothing. The right arm was little better. No major arteries appeared torn or severed. At least I didn't see any blood spurting out of his body. I was grateful. Ron was alive and not hopelessly bleeding out. A tough old bastard.

"Oh shit, oh fucking dear," he uttered and looked at his watch, which miraculously remained on his wrist. "There goes Happy Hour at Ray's." He began moaning, his eyes glassy and barely responsive. I made pressure bandages by ripping up my shirt. Then wound the remaining fabric around his head. As I sheltered him from the wind with my body, I kept firm pressure at the puncture sites of both breaks, and prayed that Qualls had secured help, help that needed to get here fast if Ron was to survive.

I cradled his head in my lap and muttered a mantra over and over of "Hang in there buddy. Hang in there buddy."

I chanted those four simple words until an Alert Air Ambulance helicopter landed nearby an eternity later. I remember loud engine noise, the dust kicked up by the rotors and the sound of humans shouting in a controlled fashion back and forth. I sort of remember three paramedics securing and loading Ron on the helicopter and lifting off. After that, thankfully, things faded to black-out, like a few drunks I've had.

***

A week later I was sitting at Ron's bed side in a private hospital room. He'd lived through the emergency surgery, a lot of transfused blood and was now buzzing away on a morphine drip. His eyes looked drugged out but he was amazingly coherent all things considered.

Our friend had no family other than all of us, which was not all that bad considering. Qualls, The Count, Waukonda, Mitterwald and even The Dog, at Ron's adamant request had made visits earlier today, the first time open visitation was allowed by the doctor in charge. The talk was brief along the lines of "Get better soon." We'd have the long winter to dissect all that had happened in the past couple of months. That's what Happy Hour at Ray's was for.

The doctor, a former surgeon in the Afghanistan war, said he'd seen worse, but those cases usually involved corpses. Both the leg and arm would be functional following some more surgery and extensive, gruelling physical therapy, but he'd probably walk with a limp for the duration and never throw a 95 mph fastball again. So much for being a "five tool player" anymore. No internal or brain injuries but Ron's body was a gloomy rainbow of black, blue, purple, yellow, and green bruises, and red-brown abrasions. One eye was still swollen nearly shut. Other than that he was fine.

"Well, we got the bastard."

"Nearly killed yourself and wrecked your plane in the process you crazy son-of-a-bitch."

"No problem. I'll buy another. Money's no object for a well-healed derelict. I could use a smoke and a big drink but I've been told I have to wait for a few more weeks. What a way to dry out."

No problem. Just buy another plane. What's $125,000 give or take? I let the matter of net worth and finances go for another time. I filled him in on what had gone down since the airplane head on out on the high lonesome bench that windy, insane afternoon. Lester's burned remains were now at the state medical examiner's in Helena. Preliminary examination revealed death by massive head trauma. His blood alcohol level was .14, not all that bad for Montana. A high level of Ritalin was also found. The Fokker was little more than charred parts including the twin machine guns and the engine. A large strip of fuselage fabric with the silver dragon nearly intact had been salvaged. Dirt laid claim to it and was planning to drape it on one of the walls at Ray's. An odd, grisly memento of sorts. The ranch was now a crime scene and closed to everyone except investigators. The place was to be put up for auction when all of this was cleared up according to a distant and quite old family member in Milk River, Alberta. Yellowstone Park at Mammoth was back to normal following the near panic stampede of tourists when the Park rangers efficiently ordered and shepherded everyone away from the potential attack site. No injuries. No damage. Merely minor mayhem. The press had descended on Biederbeck like a herd of hyenas and made life miserable for all of us. I'd nearly decked one hot shit network news reporter, a clown with silvery hair wearing a safari jacket, and his cameraman, too, but Dirt had pulled me inside his place avoiding certain legal complications. With a week passed since the death of Lester and nearly every angle of the murders had been dissected ad nauseum by the inbred television talking heads. How many hours can these idiots spend talking about the flight characteristics of a Fokker D.VII? Ron and his doctor refused to have any truck with these bottom feeders. So gradually they all packed up and moved on to the next bloody story. Useless, every one of them. Life was slowly returning to its slightly arcane and charmingly eccentric form of normal around here. All of us had been interrogated, grilled, debriefed, treated like low lives by every law enforcement agency known to man including the state police, the FBI, and Homeland Security. Even Qualls, Mitterwald and the rest of the county's law force had been worked over. Nothing came of this. Lester killed nine men using a World War I fighter and now he was dead. Since none of us were complicit in any of this and guilty of only trying to preserve our community, and maybe a decent dose of naiveté and stupidity, no charges were issued for anyone including Lester. Can't hang a dead man. There was some talk of making a movie of the whole sad mess, but nobody around here was in the least bit interested, money or no, or inclined to give such a project the time of day. Hollywood shenanigans held no interest for us.

Ron listened, thought for a couple of minutes, then asked one question of one word, "Why?"

"Beats the hell out of me. He'd completed the reconstruction of the Fokker that his father began decades ago. And, well, I guess crazy ideas fly into our heads out of the blue. Maybe the drug death of his brother flipped him out. Maybe the lonesome ranch life. I don't know. But he was a killer and a psychopath. I'm glad he's dead."

Ron squeezed the morphine drip and began to fade away.

"Could be he was just an evil bastard whose time here was meant to teach us that evil is real and that the rest of us should be humbly grateful that we're not," and he drifted off to sleep.

Good versus evil. I was beginning to believe that much of life was just that simple.

About the Author

John Holt is the author of 22 published books including *Stalking Trophy Browns, Montana Fly Fishing Adventures, Yellowstone Drift – Floating the Past in Real Time, Arctic Aurora – Canada's Yukon and Northwest Territories, Hunted: A Novel, Coyote Nowhere – In Search of America's Last Frontier*, and *Fly Fishing Adventures – Montana*. His work has appeared in such publications as *Men's Journal, Fly Rod & Reel, The Denver Post, American Cowboy, Audubon, Jeep Magazine, Big Sky Journal, E – The Environmental Magazine, Art of Angling Journal*, and *Outside*. He and his wife, photographer Ginny Holt, live in Livingston, Montana.

www.newpulppress.com